MR SYMMINGTON
MYSTERIES: CASE 001
HANDS OF TIME

BY: COREY HOWARD

ABOUT THE AUTHOR

If there is one thing that I can tell anyone about myself is that the cool colours describe me the best. My reason is that I'm a cool hearted person by nature, but have a fierce passion for creativity. This is why I fell in love with writing because it the foundation of the creative spirit and anyone who embraces it will have wonderful stories to tell. Finally, I will leave you with one of my inspirational messages. "Always be inspired by you and what makes you smile."

P.S I sing when I am happy. I'm laughing.

Acknowledgment For
Mr Symmington Mysteries: Case 001 "Hands of Time"

The list of persons that I have to thank might just take up the whole page, or be another novel altogether. And with that said, I would love to thank one of my closest friends, well more of a sister to me Ms Rhona Smith for taking the time out to read Mr Symmington's first mystery case and loving it. Also I would like to thank God for his amazing gift to me.

Others would include:

Chattel House Publishing

My Family & Friends

Renee' Best

ISBN 978-976-96126-0-0 eBook

Published by Corey Howard

Email Address: chowey175@gmail.com

Sugar Hill, St Joseph

Barbados 2018

Distribution

Chattel House Publishing

 The Belle,

St Michael, Barbados

TABLE OF CONTENTS

MR. SYMMINGTON:

HANDS OF TIME

CHAPTER 1

COTTONDALE

5TH NOVEMBER 1961 (GUY FAWKES NIGHT)

The invitations were accepted without any second thoughts given. The guests greeted their host hoping the press were close by and would camp out overnight, just to get the inside scoop on what would be the envy of all stories once told. They entered the dining room only to be amazed at the table setting décor with traditional decorations, which was the promise of a good evening.

The gathering sat to enjoy a tantalizing dinner while engaging in laughter, opinions and insights on interesting topics such as art and politics just to name a few. The host however was much more interested in the main purpose for inviting his guests as he is about to reveal a tale like none other. It will have jaws dropping to the floor for sure, thanks to the person he is glancing at continuously. His intuition caused him to invent the phrase "Hands of time" as it is his reason to carry on knowing it is long overdue. One of his guests leans over to enquire about his demeanour, as they observe him not enjoying his dessert which was of superb taste. They did however give a compliment to his hosting, and continue enjoying the evening; even laughing when a peculiar statement was made by another guest who was more excited just to be in his company.

"I hope there will be a story afterwards, as the setting is most inviting," she said holding back the anxiety she was feeling as she awaits the outcome.

"As a matter of fact, I did prepare for quite an occasion," he responded knowing they would be thrilled to hear one, which is sure to be quite unexpected.

And so our host Mr Charles Symmington drew everyone's attention when he taps his fork against his wine glass and asked his guests if they would join him in the Winselscott's living room. He instructed the hired helpers to prepare the tea and light refreshments, and then joins everyone, where he will let them in on a secret he knew for quite some time. They all sat and prepare themselves as Charles stood and looked at his three puzzle pieces which stood majestically above and on the fireplace. He too did exactly what his person of interest did when he interrupts them to ask another guest named Mrs Velda Sweetroum to stay at the dinner table, while he joins the others as she will play a part in his story.

Charles began his tale by reminding his guest about an incident in particular, letting nothing much out of the bag as it will go down as one of his favourites and how it had thought him a valuable lesson. He begins by saying how some cases are well preserved by time, thanks to the character's who perform in them and this cases is no exception.

"What do you Charles," George asks.

"I will explain after I clear up a few lose ends," Charles reply and could sense how everyone is hanging onto his every word and for certain what might be said next would cause someone to have sleepless nights, or never sleep alone again for the fear of having the culprit looking at them through the window.

Charles told his story is based on the murders which occurred six years ago and for one made the hairs on the necks of Cottondale, England stood straight. He watched as everyone was about to become hypnotize by his amazing theory, something he has grown accustom to and is more than happy to share with them. He gave the major piece of the puzzle but ask his guest to hang onto it, until he is ready to release the rest of the puzzle pieces.

"I'm referring to the murders of Elizabeth Cartridge and Peter Winselscott," he said absorbing the gasps and stunned faces before him.

He told the gathering the cases were so complex, that when he visited the death bed of former Inspector Jonathan Stonewall, it was him who gave the final major clue which help solve the case. There he reveals how the inspector wished every year before his death; he could find the whodunit, just so he could have some closure. Charles told everyone what the odd thing the inspector said which had him and his constables baffled until now.

"I thought I was going crazy, when I took a second look at it," Charles said and stops to allow the hired helpers to serve the tea and light refreshments. He smiles when his guest in the other room looks at him, then return his attention to another lady guest named Dr Christine Meredith who gave the compliment.

"You've solve the case, haven't you Mr Symmington," she said and watch as Charles turns to face the small neatly grandfather's clock which stood on the mantelpiece, along with the other two puzzle pieces and it is the perfect keeper to the secret with the passing of time.

CHAPTER 2

COTTONDALE

5th AUGUST 1955

The crime scene could only be described as chaotic with constables moving with haste to secure a horrible discovery. The body of a young woman no more than twenty-three was found dead in the nearby woods, which was just a stone throw away from the Winselscott's home. Inspector Jonathan Stonewall stared in a daze as he tried to put together what went horribly wrong, while listening to Sergeant Tommy Browning who filled him in on the statements they gathered.

Sergeant Browning started by saying a telephone call came on around one in the afternoon from Mrs Justine Meadows who lives a short distance away from the Winselscott's. He points to a middle age gentleman named Conrad Winselscott who found the girl's body while hunting peasants with his son Peter. Sergeant Browning indicates to the Inspector Stonewall that Constable John Starlight is the one who took the Conrad's statement and should have it ready by the end of the proceedings.

Inspector Stonewall came to understand the young woman's name is that of Elizabeth Cartridge who hasn't been seen since yesterday afternoon. She usually goes for late evening walks, before returning home to prepare for work the next day. Inspector Stonewall asked what her employment was and is told she is a secretary at Circus Balloon factory and have to take the 5 o'clock to get to work on time in London. Jonathan shook his head and inquire as to who raised the alarm of the missing woman.

Tommy informed him it was the girls' mother who came to the station and reported her daughter missing and made it clear she had no enemies or followers of any kind. What Sergeant Browning said next would rip Inspector Stonewall's guts right out of his body, when he said Elizabeth's mother also stated her daughter was saving herself for marriage even though she wasn't a devoted Christian.

"Did you notice anything odd Sergeant Browning?" Inspector Stonewall asked

"What's that sir?"

"Never mind," Stonewall replied then told it will be left to the corners and the inquest to give the public some in depth about the matter. He then told Sergeant Browning he is finished here as there is nothing left but paper work, which is the part he'd rather miss.

Sergeant Browning shouted to the coroners to take the body but after allowing the photographer a couple closer up shots, so he could have a better look at the office which might prove helpful. He follows Inspector Stonewall over to Conrad Winselscott where they ask him to go over the events of the afternoon. Conrad looked to his son Peter and told Inspector Stonewall he brought him along for company then asks if he can take Peter home as his mother gets worried when Peter isn't home on time for dinner. Inspector Stonewall in turn looks to Sergeant Browning who nods his head saying it would be fair and so gave the okay, which Conrad was happy to comply with.

Conrad agreed and began to relive the exact same story he told Constable Starlight. He outlines how he and his son Peter came into the woods looking for wood for the fireplace pointing to the axe in the distance. It was there Inspector Stonewall notice a gun alongside the axe and immediately asks Conrad two questions. First he asked why the gun was brought along as Cottondale looks rather peaceful and secondly had the gun being fired recently.

"I brought the gun for protection," Conrad replied then told the inspector something rather interesting which is the gun has been fired recently. "We usually come quite early in the morning and were lucky to get a few, weren't we my son," Conrad told but Peter just stood there withdrawn from everything around him. He also told them his wife will be preparing a treat for the family with one of her peasants' recipes.

Even though what Conrad said might just place him as the leader on the suspects list along with his son, Inspector Stonewall somehow believes the old chap and gave the okay to leave. He did however stress to Conrad he would expect him to gave further details as he will continue to give interviews on the case, as well as having both of them present at the inquest. Conrad on the other hand couldn't believe his luck and was stunned to understand why he was fortunate to have this ordeal happen to him instead of someone else.

"Inspector nothing like this has ever happened before in Cottondale," Conrad said.

Inspector Stonewall stops then turns to Conrad and told him he should be more aware as anything goes as the world turns. He also mentions to Conrad to allow his men to search for the truth, followed by asking where he can find the nearest phone. He got the easiest answer for the evening when Conrad states he could go to Mrs Meadow's home by passing his family's own. Sergeant Browning agreed but wondered if Peter appeared to have a medical condition of some sort. Inspector Stonewall thanks both gentlemen then turn to Sergeant Browning to take him to Mrs Meadows where he can make the deserving call.

CHAPTER 3

SMARTS VILLAGE 29ᵀᴴ JULY 1960

Ms Jean Kalthrough arrives at the prompt time of 7:45 am to begin her daily job as caretaker and sometimes stay in companion to Mrs Gwyneth Tallbottom. She enters and heads directly to the kitchen, where she puts on the kettle then made her way to the master bedroom, only to find Gwyneth sitting up in bed and reading the newspaper. Gwyneth an elderly woman said her good mornings instantly once she saw Jean came through the door. Jean returns the greeting and stares briefly at Mrs Tallbottom and thanks her lucky stars for their twenty age difference, hoping never to gain Mrs Tallbottom's state of misery.

Gwyneth made the remark telling Jean it appears she doesn't like the gift a grandfather's clock she gave her last Christmas. Jean responds by saying she hasn't gotten around to finding a place for the thing, but will see to it over the coming weekend. She got right to work by folding some clothes from yesterday's laundry, changing the subject by enquiring what interest the newspaper has in, that has alerted Gwyneth.

Gwyneth gave her the long version starting with the young lad Tommy who came up with the paper, not letting Jean forget about Tommy's mother Velda who helps every now and again. She said his mother gave him the key to come in and in his hand was the newspaper.

"I didn't ask you all that Mrs Tallbottom,"

"But I must tell you," Gwyneth replied then went on about how responsible Tommy is and how much of a good husband he will be to the girl he marries. She finally got around to Jean's question and told how she was reading the courts, only to discover the upcoming murder trial of Bentley Wright. The accused man will be in court for strangling his wife, then placing a rosary in her hand after he tidies her up. She also told how his defence is going to refer it to some mental disorder which might go well with the jury.

"Who will be the presiding judge," Jean ask

"I wish it could be the blood hound himself. Mr Symmington," Gwyneth told even betting her life's fortune the blood hound would have the answer in no time. She drifted from what she was about to say next only to ask Jean if she is quite a bit of a clumps after witnessing Jean dropping some of the laundry she held in her hand. "They were too much to carry Mrs Tallbottom, no wonder they fell out of my hand," Jean told

After picking them up Jean opens the window allowing the sunlight to fill the room and got right back to her task. Gwyneth returns to the topic by saying the case is going to be interesting none the less, hoping the presiding judge doesn't accept the defence accusations. She did however state if the judge was Charles

Symmington he would be doing his homework before giving both the defence and the prosecution a good logical whipping with his theory.

"So sorry he went into retirement early, how sad," Gwyneth said

"Mr Symmington should have been a detective instead, by now he would be the police commissioner," Jean said jokily.

"It would be all thanks to his strict parents, the force needs someone like him," Gwyneth said.

Their discussion was short lived when Tommy's mother Velda Sweetroum walks in and instantly said her morning greetings. She gave her reason for coming over which was Tommy forgot to bring home the dinner basket, as she will need it to bring Gwyneth's supper later on. Her memory quickly jolted her in telling Jean the kettle was on and she took it upon herself to turn it off.

"That's alright," Gwyneth said

"I owe you one Velda," Jean told.

Velda apologizes for interrupting their conversation and was glad to know it was about what interest caught Mrs Tallbottom eyes. She took it from there by asking if any of them had the chance of reading the obituaries, as it would be of interest to Gwyneth.

"Give me a minute while I take a look," Gwyneth said and quickly flips through until she came to the obituaries. She used her finger to guide her until she found what Velda was talking about and read the small column which to her appeared to be a daily announcement.

She took off her glasses and told it is a shame what happen to the poor girl named Elizabeth Cartridge, sympathizing with her parents about starting a tradition. The tradition was to place Elizabeth death in the papers every year, so that society wouldn't forget about her. She then asks Velda if Elizabeth's obituary was the one she was referring to.

"Why yes it is," Velda replied also agreeing with Mrs Tallbottom about the sadness the girl's death reaped. She then turns to Jean that was all caught up with her chores, and asks if she remember that awful day. Jean told her she vaguely remembered the girl's death and continue onwards with placing the last of the clothing into the draws.

"Peter Winselscott," Gwyneth said and this caught both Velda and Jean's attention. She remembers the young man face a much similar fate, and how the village look at a guy named Steven Fairbanks to answer for his murder. Velda quickly caught on and told how the police never could tie him to the murder and again ask Jean if she remembers.

"I don't think so, I was in America at that time," Jean said then told she will go and prepare the tea inviting Velda to have a cup with them.

She stops in her tracks when Gwyneth asks Velda if she ever wondered what happen to the boy's mother, then left to return with the tea. Gwyneth and Velda continued on saying how the police also found themselves baffled as to what might have happen. She also told how it was the boy's father who found Peter's body and said it must have been the most dreadful thing one can encounter.

"It's a mystery to us all Mrs Tallbottom," Velda said

"Except for one person,"

"Who Mrs Tallbottom,"

"The blood hound himself, I wondered if the police sought him out with the details," Gwyneth told. She quickly asks why he didn't take up the case and brought the rat out of the bag with his clues disguise as cheese bait.

"Don't be silly Gwyneth, Mr Symmington has been in retirement for almost a year or there about," Velda said and laughed.

Gwyneth wasn't sympathetic as she told Velda, Charles should have continued with his work as he stands for true justice among England's elite. She also told how Mr Symmington is quite selfish, stating he isn't the only man in the world to have lost his wife quite early. Velda stood in the blood hound's corner saying Mr Symmington just needed a break before returning to what he does best.

Jean returns with the tea tray and a few crackers, so that Mrs Tallbottom could nibble on, while she prepared the true breakfast. She didn't enquire what the two were talking about while she wasn't there, but told Gwyneth she will set the bath water for her shower. Velda took her queue and told them she must be getting a head start and bid them both a good day. She did however invite Jean to her home so that she could fill her in on the juicy details about the two murders.

"I will take you up on that offer," Jean said and watched Velda make her exit.

"I hope you do," she also heard and turns to Mrs Tallbottom who was now taking her first sip of tea. Jean then smiled to herself at the witty elderly lady, who should have been a journalist with her cunning face.

CHAPTER 4

5TH SEPTEMBER 1960

Inspector Jonathan Stonewall waited patiently with George Ellsworth for Charles to make his appearance down the stairs of his home in Chalfont St Peter in Buckinghamshire. They were told by Chadwick; Charles wouldn't be long as he is looking forward to a restful and relaxing day. Until then the two carried on their own conversation with Jonathan asking George, if he did the favour he ask of him the other day. George told without hesitation he hasn't find the right time to ask Charles as he is beginning to get use to his new chapter in life and all.

"Try to understand George, Charles has all the time in the world now that he is retired," Jonathan said

"Yes I agree but Charles only lost his wife a month ago, and his retirement has now started," George replied

"I hope both of you are here to comment on my chosen look," Charles said as he came down the stairs fixing his shirt which was a first to him. He is usually fitted in jacket and tie with intensions of sending some criminal to reminisce on what he has done.

Jonathan took his chance even though the stare from George told him to hold off for the moment. He asks Charles as they follow him into his study if he so happened to read about his on-going investigation. Charles said yes as he read today's paper which contains the girl's memoriam. He also told he is following closely the murder trial of Bentley Wright who is accused of murdering his wife around the same time. George cut in and asks if there aren't any leads which he could follow.

"We were looking at one person in particular but it led me to a dead end," Jonathan said

"I agree with you Inspector Stonewall," Charles said while admiring the view from his window. He turns and told them he figured it was what George and Jonathan were discussing before he came down stairs. George confesses telling he advised Jonathan he isn't sure Charles would be interested.

"I know that George but things aren't going the way I thought," Jonathan confesses.

He asks Charles to reconsider even saying how the commissioner is making his life miserable with harassment about solving the bloody cases. He even told it might have taken a toll on his health as he has a doctor's appointment later in the afternoon. He gave one more push saying it would help if the blood hound could weigh in on the matter. Charles shook his head before casting a glance in George's direction. He agrees the case does have some serious gaps which truly need some insight then told he has made a decision. He watches as the two waited with panting breath like those of a criminal who has been found guilty by the jury.

"I will help you Inspector Stonewall, but I will need to know everything," Charles said and invite both men to have a seat.

Inspector Stonewall began revealing his evidence by telling Charles his chief is placing pressure on him for finding closure for both murders. George asks if he also means the murder of Peter Winselscott who faced a much similar fate like that of Elizabeth Cartridge. Jonathan admitted the two murders are quite strange and continued on. He took from his jacket a paper article confessing how it adds salt to his wounds every year as the cases goes unsolved.

Charles took the paper and read the article with his monocle. He asks Jonathan to give some insight into what led Scotland Yard to believe Steven Fairbanks was the cause for such horrible crimes. Jonathan told him the police are still trying to piece anything together which might link Steven to the killings. He also told how Steven Fairbanks was released from prison around the same time, which was a good place to start.

"I see," Charles said and continued "So to you nothing seems to be adding up,"

"That's the hard part Charles, sorry Mr Symmington," Jonathan said but was told there is no need to apologize, as Charles likes to be called by his first name.

Charles then enquires about the person who found the bodies and asks if nothing odd struck out about the findings. Inspector Stonewall challenge Charles's question asking why a father would have reasons to kill his own son. He further told Conrad hardly knew Elizabeth so it was only logical to cross him off the list of suspects. He gave a detail sketch of Conrad who was very distraught when he found his son's body with the bullet hole to the head. George score points when he asks what might be the number one question, which was, where did Conrad find his son's body? Then look at Charles.

"Peter's body was found in the exact same place as the girl's and no one can indicate where a killer places his or her victims," Inspector Stonewall said.

Charles nods his head agreeing with the statement made by Jonathan. He understood what the inspector was trying to say then asks the Inspector what it is he felt happen. Both listen as Jonathan gave his account of what might have occurred. He told Steven Fairbanks is indeed the culprit as he just came from prison, after spending seven years then went home to his mother's. It was there that Steven Fairbanks made a proposal to Elizabeth, who turned him down and he killed her.

"What about Peter," Charles asked

"I believe Steven found out Peter had saw it and led him into the woods where he killed him because of his medical condition, leaving his mark as a killer by placing Peter's body on the same spot as Elizabeth," Jonathan replies

"Medical condition," George asked

"Yes it was rumoured throughout Cottondale that Peter Winselscott acted strange and withdrawn and would only venture out with his father Conrad," Jonathan told and continued "However Charles my investigation proves I have nothing to tie Steven to the crime, he is living a happy life," Jonathan said

Charles was amaze by Jonathan's theory as it wraps itself around the odd occurrences. He then asks if Steven still resides at his mother and if no, where is his place of residence, as he might be interested in talking with him. Inspector Stonewall confirms Steven still lives home with his mother which is in Cottondale, where the murders occurred. He also told how Steven took up farming growing produce on a piece of land his father left him.

George quickly mentions he knows someone in Cottondale a solicitor named Jeremiah Blackworth. He reminds Charles how he would spend his summers up there when Charles visited his aunt. Charles agrees but had one outstanding question.

"I wondered what really started this whole mess," Charles said

"That is a relief for me Charles, I'm glad you have reconsidered," Inspector Stonewall said. He then told both George and Charles he must be going as he doesn't want to be late for his appointment. He did invite Charles to look into the matter and he has already instructed his constables to assist him in any way they can. He then told them he would see himself out and left Charles and George to fill in the gaps which needed closing.

After Jonathan left Charles rocks back into his chair then stares at George who then asks what it is he is thinking about. Charles didn't say anything right away as he felt the inspector might have another assumption but didn't want to say. He did however tell George he can would into the case but from at home. His reason is he is now starting to get over his wife's death and adapting to his new way of life.

"What are you saying Charles,"

"I'm saying you may have to take the lead on this one George," Charles said and continued. He told George he would have to use his methods to access all clues necessary, and then report back to him when he would place the pieces in the right slot. He also gave another reason which is he wants to follow the murder trial of Bentley Wright as something didn't seem right with the way the prosecution is handling the case.

"Somehow he is going to be found guilty George," Charles said then told George he must get a move on if he is to get a sniffing head start.

CHAPTER 5

23ᴿᴰ MARCH 1956

Jane Winselscott climbs the stairs of her spring time set cottage, after returning from her husband's funeral. She stood in the middle of the bedroom unable to move, but felt the pearls around her neck with her hands, while taking a good look at the room. She stops when she saw herself which was drench in black from head to toe and that's when it finally hits her. She closed her eyes then opens them only to see the bed they slept in and visualize the final ordeal before the angel of death came into town.

She remembers lying next to Conrad having a conversation on the bridge game they had the other evening with the Archers. She told she couldn't believe they lost the final trick at last minute and blames herself for them losing the game. Conrad told her not to worry herself as the rematch is scheduled for Saturday afternoon.

"Oh Conrad you know how sorry I am," she said and sat up in bed.

Conrad took no notice and instead turns on his left side and started to relax, so that he could drift into slumber land. He wouldn't get far as he felt Jane's elbow shoving him to turn over. Conrad asks in a frustrated tone of voice what seems to be the matter and waited for a response. Jane told him she wanted to talk and when asks what about she hesitated. She knew her husband's short temper and came quickly out with the nagging thought of what are they going to do for the anniversary death of their son Peter in September.

Conrad instantly said it is going to be like last time where they would take flowers to his grave. What Jane said next made him sat straight up in bed. She told him it has been a year since his death and she wants to do something special. Conrad drown out whatever was said next as he too remembers that awful day. He remembers going for wood to bring home when he discovers a horrific scene, and longs to forget. He came too after he heard Jane say she wants to hold a vigil in his honour.

"Why?"

"Because he deserves it that's why," she told then begins to cry.

Conrad took her into his arms and began to comfort her. Through her sobs Conrad heard how much his wife missed their son. To him it is the worst possible pain any parent can face. He kisses her on the forehead and told how everything is going to be fine, then pleas for her to get some sleep. Jane finally agrees but had one more question on her mind and prays that Conrad would give her a suitable answer.

"How did we go blind Conrad, it wasn't what we expected," she said.

Conrad couldn't answer but instead repeat something his mother told him on the day his father died when he was twenty-one. He said his mother got up and picks up her watch and stares at it, before looking at him without a tear in her eye.

"If life had presented us with an hour glass, our lives would be worth much living," (the voice of Conrad's mother.)

Again he kisses her then told they will talk about it in the morning. The next morning her worse fears came to pass when Jane called Conrad for his breakfast. She didn't get an answer and decided to take the stairs to get him out of bed if by force. Once she enters the bedroom, Conrad's mother's words came back to haunt her.

"Oh Conrad," she calls out to him as the chinning of the clock brought her back to life. She stares at the bed which reminded her of being the only occupant from now onwards. She exited the room and makes the trip down stairs, but stood frozen when she saw it and all that she lost came back to her.

CHAPTER 6

COTTONDALE: 8TH SPETEMBER 1960

George's car made the left turn off the main road and begun its half mile drive journey towards Jeremiah Blackworth's manor. Instantly he had flash backs of the time he spent, mostly his first few weeks of summer at the enormous manor, if it remains the same. No one can forget Jeremiah's strict parents who narrowed down his circle of friends to just one, and one of their choosing of course. How George became the lucky one even he had to guess but his time was well spent, as the two boys played just about every game they could think of.

His car approaches the manor and he couldn't believe nothing has changed in almost twenty years since his last visit. He saw Jeremiah standing in the distance and was his official greeting once he steps out of the car. Of course George made a joke by reminding Jeremiah about the lesson his parents thought him, which is to be the invitation as it shows good hospitality spirits.

"Well they had to taught me something, how are you old chap," Jeremiah said jokily

"Quite tiresome from the long drive, I must say," George replied.

"Well I have some wonderful treats to your liking, come follow me," Jeremiah told and led the way.

Along the way he told George how marvellous it is to finally see him after all these years and how long has George been solving crime. "About five years now," George said and he too returns the friendly comment. He also told the blood hound is doing even better now that he is out of the court room and is free to medal in police business as always. Jeremiah laughs and led George into his entertaining quarters where lunch has already been prepared.

As they eat the two filled in each other on their families where George was please to know Jeremiah's children had all grown up and were doing fine for themselves. His youngest child Jacqueline had recently gotten married to the new Earl of Wingover William Fairchild III and had two beautiful daughters. George matched his friend by saying his son Clearance had been happily married for almost a year now to the daughter of Dame Thornberry, who loved to be the sword of outspokenness.

"What seems to bring you around George, if you don't mind my asking?"

"I'm on a special assignment," George told and hoped Jeremiah brought his crazy explanation.

Jeremiah didn't buy it though, instead his sixth sense told him otherwise. He cut right to the chase and ask George if he is there to investigate someone or something. George had to agree with his friend, and blames it on hanging around Mr Symmington for way too long. He figures since the cat is out of the bag, he might as well tell

Jeremiah what his intentions are. He claims to be on the hunt for anything which can shed light on the double murders some five years ago.

"You mean the murders of Elizabeth Cartridge and Peter Winselscott?"

"Why yes to be precise, can you tell me anything Jeremiah," George told.

Jeremiah straightens himself in his chair then folds his hands before starting. He first told George he is too familiar with the way the blood hound works and it is showing in George. With that said he told from the little knowledge he knows it might not help George in his quest to find an answer.

"Let me be the judge of that," George told and waited patiently for Jeremiah to begin.

He starts by telling George the murders were quite imaginary as he would never guest someone could be so cruel. He went on about the news surrounding Peter's murder and found it quite unsettling, as Peter mostly stood by himself giving George an example.

"Do you remember Cottondale's annual fair?"

"Of course you drag me to it every year during our young summers," George replied seeing Jeremiah's board smile.

"Well I believe it was at last year's fair," Jeremiah begun and went on. He told him the theme for last year was the re-enactment of King James I heroic capture of Guy Fawkes and it was there he noticed the shy and lonely Peter. His major observation was the way how Peter stood by himself, as no one would ask him to join in the festivities.

"How come," George ask

"I can't really say George, but if I was a doctor, I would diagnose him as having severe anxiety," Jeremiah told.

George was quite amused with his friend's statement knowing he was not a general practitioner. However, he cast it aside as he wanted a bit more on his plate. He wanted Jeremiah to carry on as what was mentioned earlier would only tickle the blood hound's taste buds, if he were here just to observe. The only interest Jeremiah could cough up was that Peter lives five houses away from the murdered girl Elizabeth, but three houses away from the police number one suspect Steven Fairbanks.

"You could talk to Ms Anita Flawington; she is very close to the parents of the decease, well at least one of them."

"Why one of them,"

"She is the village baker George, hasn't Charles told you anything," Jeremiah said while laughing. He gave a brief insight on Anita giving credit to her tasty and freshly baked loaves. He really caught George interest when he said how Ms Flawington would fill him in on the gossip around town, thanks to the generous favours of the gossip sisters.

"Gossip sisters,"

"Yes, but we will get to them eventually," Jeremiah said.

George learnt that last Friday Jeremiah paid a visit to Anita and was given and earful. Anita told him Peter's mother left a year ago to live with her sister Wanda Chestnut in Cheshire after her husband died.

"Really,"

"Quite. He was the one to have found them both you know," Jeremiah said and wasn't too surprized at George's quick thinking when he asked if Inspector Stonewall knew about it. Jeremiah wasn't sure but stated Conrad, Peter's father never regained himself both mentally and physically. He hits George towards the cricket boundaries when he states it isn't the first time Peter's family went through such an ordeal.

"Peter's uncle committed suicide when he was just thirty-one, how dreadful," Jeremiah said. He also claims up to present time no one can say for certain what the circumstances were for the young man who took his own life.

George shook his head understanding what was being said to him it's the fuel which lights Charles's curiosity. He did however switch the topic so he wouldn't bore his friend to pieces, but truthfully he figures Ms Flawington would know more than what meets the eye. He asks Jeremiah if he had any love interest as of late and was surprize to hear Jeremiah indeed had one but misfortune had other plans in store.

"What Happened?"

"She died George," Jeremiah said and stares blankly across the room. He did however confess it truly got lonely sometimes but he has his grandchildren to pass the time with.

George could understand where Jeremiah was coming from as he and Charles as of late were experiencing the same scenario. He even watched Charles lose interest in his passion the fight for justice after his wife died, and only came back to town just a few days ago. He heard

Jeremiah mention a proposal where the two of them along with Charles should take a night on the town which is sure to be a hit.

"George I am quite sure you and Charles are two well respectable gentlemen, so the ladies have no fear," Jeremiah said and begin to laugh.

"That would be a change," George said but came up with the idea of inviting Jeremiah to tag along with him as he pays a visit to Ms Flawington. Jeremiah accepts without giving a second thought, which to him is something out of his particular realm.

CHAPTER 7

9TH SEPTEMBER 1960

It was Charles's turn to get to work. After all it would be fair to George who already was getting enough insight as it is. From what was told to him on Inspector Stonewall's second visit; Charles sat in the library, going through some medical books. He was hoping to find some interesting details on his research of a certain subject. He turns the page after writing something valuable down, when he came across some information that spelt out everything for him.

Taking the notes Charles began to wonder about Jonathan's concern when he visited him the next day after George left. It was there Jonathan really told Charles what he thought, even gave his own diagnosis, but left Charles to clarify which he was doing right about now. In the mix of his work a beautiful woman approached his table. She had eyes that resembles green emeralds and long red hair, but with very few noticeable freckles.

"I hope you don't mind if I join you," she said

"Of course you may," Charles replied and watches her take the seat opposite his. At first he thought she wanted to borrow one of his books, but was thrown back when she confessed about wanting to join him from the moment she realized he was the blood hound himself.

"My name is Dr Christine Meredith," she told

"Then I am him, who says I am," Charles responded with a smile on his face.

Christine apologizes for interrupting his study and read the title of the book. Charles confesses his research is based on a hunch given to him by someone looking for answers. Christine turns the book towards her, read the topic, and then boldly told him she too has been doing research for years on the particular subject.

"I am a professor at Cambridge, teaching my specialty and the importance of it, to fourth year medical students," she told.

Christine enlightens Charles about her in depth knowledge on the subject and wouldn't mind sharing and discussing some of his findings. Charles was very impress with his library acquaintance and wanted to know more about her. Christine gave a little insight into her personnel life, by jokily saying she is currently house sitting for her parents, who are also doctors.

"They are in South Africa trying to lower the high percentage of malnourish cases in children," she told.

"I see,"

"And I have a younger brother named Donovan,"

Christine claims to be very fortunate thanks to the wonderful help of Ms Dorothy Twinkleton, who specializes in giving care to special children of that order. However, her Donovan wasn't a child he is twenty-two. Charles gave a little knowledge about himself, despite he didn't need to. He is already well known, Christine said it herself when she referred to him as the blood hound. To say it briefly Christine already did her work on Charles Symmington.

"Why a beautiful woman such as you aren't married, or at least engaging in some usual courting ritual?" Charles asks

"I haven't come across the man that can quench my appetite; furthermore, my brother is my top priority," Christine responded.

She did however felt a little embarrass by boldly asking Charles if he would like to come to dinner. Charles wanted to decline, but Christine insistence caused him to think otherwise. His reason was what she offered at the end, and no it wasn't intimacy. It was the invitation to further discuss the topic which he is researching in front of him.

The two continued their conversation for a messily two minutes, when Christine states she has to run off to teach her 2:30 pm class. She did however promise to hurry home right after her class, which was more be a tutorial than anything else.

"I will call the cook to let her know I am having guest around seven," she told then dashes off like a cowboy following the trail of the sunset.

Charles watches her leave before being caught by the librarian supervisor, who only smiles at him. He did cast his blanket of self-conciseness through the window as he returns to his research, which will be quite interesting to discuss with Dr Meredith. He places down his pen only to ask himself why Jonathan didn't say what he concluded from the beginning. It would shed light on the matter and explains why he couldn't arrest Steven Fairbanks.

"Are you getting through Mr Symmington?" the librarian supervisor asked.

"Yes I am I was just thinking," Charles said and carried on with his research when he also remembered what Jonathan told him on his second visit.

"I didn't want him to know of my suspicions Charles, that's why I came back," Charles recalls.

CHAPTER 8

6:45 PM 9TH SEPTEMBER 1960

Dorothy Twinkleton prepares herself for dinner while she glances at Donovan, every now and again, just to see what he is up to. She couldn't help but admire his stocky male structure, looking adorable like a teddy bear at the window. She never bothered to wonder why he didn't have any friends, wait that's a lie I told him does have one friend, more like a companion. He talks to a glass of water which I am surer is the only thing he trusts in the world.

"Donavan," she calls

"Yes,"

"I except you to be on good behaviour, as your sister has an important guest arriving soon,"

"I promise to be," he said then started laughing for no apparent reason. It appears he witness something funny while looking through the window. His amusement came in the form of the gardener just trimming the hedges, and this made Dorothy love her new job even more.

She stops her admiration after her fingers rested slightly on the vanity table. There she touched a piece of paper displaying the obituary reading of Mrs Gwyneth Tallbottom who passed away three years ago. She recalled how divested she was when she received the call from an acquaintance of hers.

Somehow her memory got the better of her, after realizing Donavan had his own entertainment going for him through the window. It all begins with the funeral of Elizabeth Cartridge. Her mind reconstructs a vivid picturesque setting where everyone present listens to the pastor's sermon. In detail the pastor told about the life of the young girl, as if he was narrating one of National Geographic documentaries. He took it further at the graveside and it was there Dorothy got a right earful from two women in particular. According to the word they are known as the gossip sisters Lattima Donahue and Rachel Rocksoft.

It was Rachel who started the conversation by saying how sorry she felt for the poor girls' mother. Her mother looks a though she is about to fall apart at any given minute. Lattima agrees but came straight out wanting to know, who did such an unforgettable act.

"I wouldn't be surprise if they arrested Steven Fairbanks. He is the mark of a pure beast Rachel," Lattima told

"Be careful Lattima the coppers are over there," Rachel said pointing to Inspector Stonewall. She did however notice the inspector didn't look as cheerful as when he met them the first time.

Lattima confirms what Rachel said but gave her own theory as to who the ideal person is, should Inspector Stonewall run a drift with the investigation. Again Dorothy looks in their direction and nearly lost her balance as she saw who they were referring to. She couldn't believe they were looking at Jeremiah Blackworth along with another person.

"You know the woods gets a lot of visits from that person," Lattima said

"You are quite right, I am surprized he attended the funeral," Rachel replied.

Lattima wasn't finish at all no surrey; she kept on like a stool pigeon after lunch. She states how Mr Jordan Brown told her about his suspicions, on the day she paid a visit to his store the other day.

Dorothy returns to reality when Christine asks if she didn't hear her knock and it is time for Donavan to take his medication. She watches as Christine laughs at her brother's funny tale, and told him her expectation of him at dinner.

"Ms Twinkleton why do you have that daze look? Please fetch the medication,"

"Right Dr Meredith; sorry," Dorothy replied and did what she was told.

While applying the medication Christine told her Mr Symmington has arrived, then asks her to take Donavan downstairs to meet him.

"I will join you after I am dressed,"

"Right Dr Meredith," Dorothy said

Before she left the room Christine ask her a very peculiar question. Dorothy's only reply is she was just thinking of a woman name Jane Winselscott, whom she hadn't heard of in quite a while. "You know how memories find their way back into your thoughts," Dorothy said

Christine agrees with the nodding of her head but cast it aside by telling they mustn't keep Mr Symmington waiting, as he might be quite hungry. The reason why she agrees is because she too drifts off every now and again, never knowing the reason why.

Once Dorothy left with Donavan to greet the guest, Christine returns to Dorothy's room and stops when it appears she had found what she is looking for. She figures she got it right after she picks up an obituary paper clipping which didn't match the person Dorothy had in mind. Instead the obituary clipping carries the name of Mrs Gwyneth Tallbottom instead of Jane Winselscott.

"Then who is Jane I wonder," Christine said to herself but cut it short after having to lie to Dorothy after she returns to her room.

"I am borrowing a pair of your earrings if you don't mind."

"Of course not Dr Meredith it's no bother at all."

CHAPTER 9

10TH SEPTEMBER 1960

George and Jeremiah arrived in time to smell the baking loaves of bread Ms Anita Flawington had in the oven. For certain they weren't going to let the opportunity pass them by, as they rang the doorbell. Anita greeted them herself at the door with her hands drench in flour from the kneading she had just finished. She was quite surprized to see Mr Blackworth at her doorstep, for no apparent reason but couldn't say the same for the man who was with him.

"Please come in," she told them and led the way into the kitchen. "Would you both like some tea and freshly baked scones, which goes well with butter and cheese?"

"Yes we would Ms Flawington, and I am happy to introduce my good friend, Mr George Ellsworth," Jeremiah said and told of George being his guest for a few days.

Anita was happy for Jeremiah, since she knew him all his life. She could testify to knowing two things about the fellow with the first of him having strict parents. The second was what everyone in Cottondale glued together, declaring his deceased wife Clara was the only friend Jeremiah ever had. Being face with George from out of the blue, Anita can now say the lonesome spell has just backfired.

"What brings you around Mr Blackworth?" she asks while sprinkling flour on the counter and continues to knead the dough.

George use one of his own methods and signals to Jeremiah to let him answer. He told Anita he used to travel to these parts, when he was much younger but wanted to know how everyone is getting along. It was enough to get Anita talking by first saying things couldn't be better.

"I blame the parliament representative Richard Locksmith for the troubling times," She began and told about everyone in the village.

She starts with Ms Lavern Rice who had just celebrated her seventieth birthday last Tuesday, and was the toast of village. Next it was the gossip sisters Rachel Rocksoft and Lattima Donahue who must be off spreading the news as usual, and advised them not to get caught up in any conversations of theirs. She placed the next set of loaves into the oven, and then puts the kettle on while mentioning how the two ladies can talk for hours on end.

She gave insight on a young couple who had just moved from Paddington, saying how they wanted some peace and quiet and went to gather the tea cups. One of the tea cups drops from her hand, but didn't suffer any damage thanks to Jeremiah's quick reflexing hands. Anita took a load off her feet and apologizes but George states it was nothing and asks if something is wrong.

"It is just every time I see that young couple Michael and Mary, I can't help but to think about poor Elizabeth Cartridge and Peter Winselscott," She said and dries her eyes with her apron. She went on to say how tragically the two past away just under five years ago.

"I thought you would have told Mr Ellsworth Jeremiah, since you attended the funerals and all," she told

"It slipped my mind," Jeremiah responded

"How could it, they were found dead in the woods, where you did your hunting on occasions," She said then cast it off. "The girl's mother still lives around here though," Anita told clarifying it is just Elisabeth's parents that are left now.

George felt like a nursery student at story time when Anita gave the backdrop on the Cartridge's. She told Elizabeth's mother married her husband Reginald just before Elizabeth was born, as the girl's real father ran off to marry his true love in Gretna Green, before making a life in London. "It was a one night encounter I understand," she told coming clean as to who spilled the honey, meaning the gossip sisters.

Ms Flawington didn't stray too far and confirms the same story Jeremiah told George. She did however go into more detail, saying how the poor girl went for a walk, only to be found later in the woods dead, after her mother Gina raised the alarm.

Jeremiah looks at George who was listening very attentively, wondering what he is thinking about and might learnt from Ms Flawington's story. He recast his attention back towards Anita just in time to hear the major part of the tale.

"It was Peter's father Conrad Winselscott who found her and Peter you know," she said then got up to take the kettle off the stove, just as it begun to whistle. "I hope you told Mr Ellsworth Peter's father past away two years ago Mr Blackworth," she said and figures she might as well finish what she started.

"How did he die Ms Flawington?" George asks

"He died in his sleep, I witnessed the death certificate," Jeremiah told.

It felt like pulling teeth to finally get Jeremiah to add to the story. She kept her thoughts to herself and went over to the fridge for the cheese and butter. She continues to make the tea, and carried on with her story, while the gentlemen help themselves to her tasty treats.

"Before you continue I must applaud you for your excellent scones," Jeremiah said reminding George how the cook used to make them for breakfast every morning. He even told they taste quite similar. George agrees with him but was much more interested in what else Ms Flawington had to say.

"I couldn't bake for at least a day when I heard what happen to Peter. It brought even more shock to Cottondale," she told. She clarifies how Peter is the son of Conrad, whose widow is living with her sister. Jeremiah mentions how he told George that much acknowledging a smirk upon Anita's face.

"You know it must be awkward to discover someone's body," she said. "Conrad must have had a nose for these things, as he too also found his son's body in the woods and in the exact place as Elizabeth," she said. She explains however Peter's parents took the news just as hard as Elizabeth parents, and couldn't face the coppers to talk as it was much too painful.

Jeremiah took it from there and told how inspector Stonewall and his constables couldn't make sense of the case. He implied how the inspector logical explanation was there had to be a lunatic on the rampage. "It took everyone by surprize," he told.

"We all thought it was Steven Fairbanks, who got out of prison just before Elizabeth's death," Anita adds

George then enquires if the inspector is still working on the case. He felt he had to scarp himself and his jaw from off the floor, from what was said next, as it was more than a surprize to him and why Charles didn't say anything is just as puzzling.

"Inspector Stonewall is suffering from a brief illness," Anita told and again got up to attend her lively hood.

"Just one other question Ms Flawington; where does Mrs Winselscott's sister reside. If you don't mind me asking? George asks

"I think she lives up in Cheshire," Anita said then asks if the two would like another scone. She didn't wait for an answer and instantly wraps two loaves of bread and some scones then gave to Jeremiah, knowing how much he likes her baking.

As for George he found out more than enough from Ms Flawington than he hoped for. He did however notice there are others he must see which includes, the gossip sister, Gina, Elizabeth's mother, Steven Fairbanks and of course Mrs Winselscott's sister in Cheshire, in order to get a good story insight on the case. He didn't just leave you know, he knew Anita was good company and indulge himself in jolly old conversations, before he took the time to enlighten Charles on what he had learnt.

CHAPTER 10

12TH SEPTEMBER 1960

Despite Charles's knee was causing him some major discomfort, he still managed his way up the stairs of his gentlemen's club. His invitation come from Anthony Adamson the youngest lordship England has ever known. He spotted Anthony who sat alone by the window with a cigar and a glass of brandy and remembers the call, which was about what Anthony read in the papers. Anthony got up and greets him after seeing Charles walk towards him in some discomfort.

"Are you alright Charles? Looks like you have some knee trouble,"

"I'm fine Anthony, I came as soon as I hung up the phone," Charles said

Anthony teases Charles saying he would be the perfect cast member to play the role of the tortoise verses the rabbit. He then signals to the waiter to bring him a deck of cards and gave the blood hound any drink he wishes. Charles ordered his favourite drink ginger vodka, and the waiter left to fill out the order. Anthony made small talk saying Charles looks happier, now that he is retired.

"I miss the bench once in a while," Charles replied.

The waiter returns with the deck of cards and Charles's drink then heads off to the next table. Anthony began to deal the cards but wasn't inviting Charles to a game of bridge. In fact, he interests himself into a game of solitaire then asks Charles where is his trustee sidekick George.

"George is in Cottondale visiting a friend of his,"

"I am surprised. The two of you are like paper and glue," Anthony joked.

Charles smiles knowing how much of a jokester Anthony is, well except when he is presiding over a case. He wanted to get Mr Adamson's view on the case which is about to make headlines all over England, the murder trial of Bentley Wright. Anthony places the cards down after he ran into difficulty from the start. He wanted to know what Charles was getting at, but knowing how Charles find valuable information, it made no sense in keeping what he thinks from Charles.

"Guilty is what I think. The jurors are going to discredit the defence theory right from the start," Anthony said. He felt Charles's concern and thought of the case of Martin Short, when the jury stunned the court with a guilty verdict. He could reminisce how the verdict shocked Charles as he was hoping they would have given Martin the lesser charge of manslaughter.

"Charles what are your intensions?" Anthony asks

"I want to see a different outcome," Charles said telling Anthony how he didn't regret having to give Martin just twenty-five years for the conviction. "I knew what would happen,"

"Of course you do Charles, you always do, but you must remember the judge must carry out what society wants," Anthony said and went on with his game. He stopped to cheer Charles up, when he told Charles about him performing excellent and extraordinary judiciary skills. It then occurs to him why Charles came to see him and it wasn't to have a friendly chat. It had to do with the fact Charles might have those same very feelings about the Bentley Wright case.

"I have to asks Charles, why has George travelled to Cottondale,"

"Elizabeth Cartridge and Peter Winselscott that's why," Charles told

Anthony knew it was strange as one is never seen without the other. He also knew it is the way Charles's work and immediately weighs in on the matter. He told Charles his assumption, where the real question is how both murders were committed and understood why the police found the cases difficult. He threw a bone Charles's way knowing quite well the blood hound will make sense of it in due course.

"For some reason, I don't know why Jeremiah Blackworth comes to mind," he told then squashed the game and began anew.

Charles was speechless by the comment; he wanted to know why his colleague would make such an accusation towards his own friend's friend. He allows Anthony to carry on after he stated he didn't really know Mr Blackworth, well not personally, as he will have to sit and listens to George after he returns from his visit. He took Charles words and went with his story. He states Jeremiah Blackworth resides in Cottondale and just like a cousin of his who is no stranger to the woods.

"To me Jeremiah seems to be a likely suspect, just like his cousin,"

"Cousin,"

"Yes, but I can't remember the name," Anthony told. "If you had any idea the history surrounding Mr Blackworth, Charles you would be the next Agatha Christie, I assure you,"

Charles also took in Anthony's logical theory about Jeremiah being the murderer, but also accepted the quick discard Anthony gave about the police never having any interest in the lonesome troll. He also made the topic more interesting when he gave an insight into his time studying law. He enlightens Charles about him going to university with one of Mr Blackworth's cousins. He laughs as he told how Jeremiah's cousin would storm out of the social gathering, when one of Anthony's friends made fun at Jeremiah whenever he came to London to visit her.

"Her?" Charles asks

"Yes, but I can't remember her name, but we call her foxy," Anthony said and laughs again but with a bit more certainty.

Charles smirks then stretches his leg out; to relieve the pain his knee was having. Again Anthony asks what the matter is and Charles states it is his knee and hasn't gotten around to seeing the doctor. Anthony couldn't believe how a man who isn't afraid to outline the steps a murderer took in committing a flawless crime, could have such horrors in seeing a doctor. He did however insist Charles sees a doctor; otherwise he might have to visit him in the hospital on some broken legs incident.

"You are afraid of the doctor telling you awful news, are you Charles," Anthony said smiling

"Keep your voice down," Charles said and smirks to amuse himself. He recast the conversation back towards Jeremiah's cousin, wanting to know if she still resides around London.

"Now that I have thought of it, I'm quite sure foxy's name is Dr Meredith,"

"Dr Christine Meredith?"

"How did you know," Anthony said and asks Charles if he knew her.

Charles confesses to knowing her but briefly, as it was she who approached him in the library just the other day. He did accept to having dinner with Dr Meredith the same very evening. His face turns a shade of bashfulness when he was tease by Anthony, who states he might just have a love interest at hand.

"It is unlikely to happen Anthony," Charles replied as he is certain the love storm has past him by.

"Give over Charles, you are quite a catch," Anthony said and places the jack of clubs, unto the queen of diamonds.

Charles figured he had gotten enough from Anthony and thanks him for his time. He tells there are places he has to visit, but cast away another outright tease about having another dinner invite from Dr Meredith. He clarified to his peer the young lady happens to like men her own age, telling Anthony he should take her up on one of her offers if necessary.

"I will take you up on that Mr Symmington, my mother is nagging me constantly about grandchildren,"

"Well do," Charles replied.

Before Charles could leave on his errands Anthony states one last thing. He told Charles he gave Martin Short the right sentence, when he gives him manslaughter's punishment. Charles asks why but Anthony only said, he saw where the police and prosecution went wrong, something all lordships should be able to detect. He also told Charles how much he idolized his work, which is the reason why he is a lordship today.

"I don't know what to say,"

"Say nothing Charles; it would only shatter the rule of law's heart even more. Recon..." Anthony stops and continues to play his solitaire, leaving Charles to wonder, while doing what he does best, as he exits his gentlemen's club.

CHAPTER 11

SMALL VILLAGE

13TH SEPTEMBER 1960

Now at the tender age of eighteen years Tommy Sweetroum has grown into quite a gentleman. He joins his parents Conliffe and Velda at the dinner table for their usual family gathering. He confirms he did wash his hands before sitting, since he spent a lot of time fixing the car, which he plans to take on the road after the summer. He felt a slap across his hand by his mother, who insists on saying grace and hands the invitation over to her husband.

"We thank you lord for what we are about to receive in our bellies, may it truly makes us thankful. Love from the Sweetroum family. Amen," Conliffe told and forgot all table manners, as he was the first to dive right into the dinner setting. He did however open the discussion around the table, by asking what his family was up to while he was hard at work.

"Nothing much from my end," Velda told

"I was with my car the whole day father. That's enough for now, I'm hungry," Tommy replied.

Marsha Tommy's older sister walks in just as the conversation was heading for a permanent stop. She brought it back to life while taking up a plate and joins the rest of the family, with a smile from ear to ear. "I have something of interest," she told, confessing she overheard her dad's open discussion after she walks through the door.

"You are such a gossip girl,"

"Shut up,"

"Quiet Tommy let your sister speak," Conliffe said and gave the floor to Marsha who took great pride in her victory, by sticking her tongue out at her bother.

Her evening began with an escort from a gentleman friend of hers named Troy. Both were about to past the old home of Mrs Tallbottom, where to her surprize there were two gentlemen she never saw before in her life.

"Did the man say who he was, Marsha?" Velda asks

"Yes he did. He said his name is Mr George Ellsworth and his friend is Mr Jeremiah Blackworth. Troy and I just look at each other," she told and went on from there. At first she wanted to make sure if he is the famous sidekick to Mr Symmington himself. She was relieved to know it was him in the flesh, almost making her want to jump right out of her skin.

Marsha knew she couldn't linger and told it was Mr Blackworth who presents his reason for arriving at the home of Mrs Tallbottom. He claims to be visiting the neighbourhood, with his friend the same very Mr Ellsworth and how they came to visit a friend of Mr Blackworth name Jean Kalthrough whom is the caretaker there. "He told he wanted to meet her if he can," Marsha said and begins to laugh.

"I wonder why no one in the village, just didn't tell them," Velda told as she became very captivated about where Marsha's story was heading.

"I thought so too, mother," Marsha told

"He should have asked," Tommy said laughing.

"Nonsense boy," Conliffe told and again asks his daughter to finish her story.

Marsha did just that by giving what the highlight of her tale was. She told Mr Blackworth that the person he wishes to see has passed away, over two years ago. She did however mention how both her mother and the lady name Ms Jean Kalthrough, looked after Mrs Tallbottom before she died. She also adds praise to Ms Kalthrough for doing such an excellent job on keeping the decease lady in high spirits. With the occasion of her mother helping with the chores every now and again.

"Ms Kalthrough doesn't live around these parts anymore," she told after Mr Blackworth asked about her. She took the nerve to ask Mr Blackworth why he didn't make visits before otherwise he would have known, but got the response that they just slipped his mind.

"You're a clever girl," Velda said and listens to what her daughter said next.

Marsha gave a history tutorial telling Mr Ellsworth how her mother came to help Ms Kalthrough tidy up the home, before Mrs

Tallbottom relatives arrived. She told her mother walked into the house only to find nothing had been done, or even started. "I told him about the single note you found mother," Marsha said and this made Velda wonder why Ms Kalthrough wasn't there when she arrived. In fact, she was much certain Jean had another day left, before she joins her sister in Cheshire.

"I remember what the note said," Velda told her family and watch her family stares at her with wide mouths open like the mouth of a cave. "I read it, before picking the paper up after only to realize, it was the same story Mrs Tallbottom was reading the day before," Velda mention with a different facial expression.

The story was so sad she couldn't read all of it Velda remembered. She told how sorry she felt for Ms Kalthrough who wrote "there is no place for her here." at the bottom of the page before signing her name. Velda turns to Tommy asking him if he remembers the day he brought the paper for Mrs Tallbottom.

"Yes ma I can't forget a thing like that," he responded. He too would add to the discussion by saying he came through the back door for the second time, and it was there he witnessed Jean wiping her tears. "She used a kitchen towel, but didn't look at me," Tommy said. He distinctively asks her if she is all right, but all she indicated was that his mother is with Mrs Tallbottom, and can join her upstairs.

"You never told me that Tommy," Velda said.

"It wasn't important at the time," Tommy replied.

To give some credit to Ms Kalthrough's character Velda states how she was a very nice woman, despite having a way of doing crazy things. She did however come to reasonable doubt that her friend wanted something worthwhile to do with her life, which is the reason why she left.

"What became of her I wonder," Velda said and told the rest to hurry up and eat their dinner, as she doesn't want to miss her favourite television show "Mack Jennings" the number one mystery shows in England.

While her family sat and watch the television Velda excuses herself and heads into the kitchen. There she took from behind the flour container and envelope with her name written on it. She quickly took out the same letter that was address to her from Ms Kalthrough, and dials the number, while looking back to see if anyone was coming her way.

"Hello,"

"Hello Jean, this is Velda can we talk,"

"Of course,"

"Okay then I will see you when you arrive," Velda said then hung up the phone after she heard her husband shout for her, telling her the show is about to start.

CHAPTER 12

16TH SEPTEMBER 1960

Gina sat by the window while the heavy down pour of rain, made it easier for her to pass the time. She didn't forget the company she has in the sitting room, which was none other than George and Jeremiah. She turns to ask them both if they would like to refill their cups of tea, taking up the tea pot to pour, but must help themselves to the tea cakes and sandwiches.

"I'm so sorry Reginald isn't here, he is much better at entertaining guest," she told

Jeremiah asks if Mr Cartridge is out of town, but didn't get a response from Gina which was quite embarrassing. Gina on the other hand asks George if he is from around these parts, as she never saw him before. George gave her the same story he gave to Ms Flawington including being the childhood friend of Mr Blackworth.

"I enjoyed spending my early weeks of summers up here," George told getting a smile from Gina's lips.

"I see; however, I notice both of you happen to be going around door to door. Is there a reason for that Mr Ellsworth?" Gina questions.

George used a method he learnt from Charles, which is to tell the client the truth, providing it brings them into their corner. It didn't work with Gina however; as she found it quite unsettling and told them; they should be restraint from nosing into other people's affairs.

"It must be about Elizabeth and Peter I gather," she told them nearly dropping her tea cup. She turns herself again to the window allowing the rain drops to inspire her to adapt composure. She heard George confess to him and the blood hound, finally having an interest in the case.

Gina looks around and took George's truth as an insult, but more of a slap in the face. "How dare you say such words Mr Ellsworth; don't you see how much time has passed?" she told. She lashed out at them both asking if they or anyone they knew; lost a child that not even Scotland Yard can propose a liable theory. "It has been five years Mr Ellsworth, five years that I have been asking myself why," she said then apologizes for her behaviour.

To George, Gina has every right to behave the way she is right now. How dare anyone take interest, when the case should have already had a court date scheduled? He guesses her biggest question is why now? If Charles Symmington is the keeper of all logical theories, then why hadn't he told England what happened, creating a thrilling story no one could ever write about. He came from his thoughts after he witnessed Gina finally come to some understanding in her mind and agrees to tell him what he came for.

She starts by insulting Inspector Stonewall who should have done better, before he came down with his illness. She stresses how tired she became with the constant repeats of the same story to the police, swearing she can recite the entire conversation to them if they wanted.

"It wouldn't be necessary Mrs Cartridge," George said then looks at Jeremiah

She looks them straight into the eyes and told them she dismissed all accusations against Steven Fairbanks, as being responsible for her daughter's death. "I assure you Mr Ellsworth, Elizabeth was a young girl when Steven went to prison. Her memory of him would be very vague,"

"What are you saying Mrs Cartridge,"

"The rumours of Steven becoming jealous of Peter and Elizabeth's love affair are sheer nonsense. Elizabeth would never love someone who acted strange. Peter always acted strange," she said.

George couldn't believe what he was hearing, how comes no one including Ms Flawington told him about Peter's strange occurrences. He places his thoughts into the back of his mind when he heard her say she have her suspicions about the killer. He asks her to say of course but learnt someone else had an interest in her daughter. From the corner of his eye he saw how uneasy Jeremiah became but knew he must see her through, otherwise he might not get this chance again.

Jeremiah on the other hand sat and watches a master at his work, despite he was quite uneasy. He observes how Gina fell helpless for George's words; especially when she was asking if Elizabeth got herself into any mischief.

"Of course not Mr Ellsworth, Elizabeth hardly left the house. Except to go for her walks," she told

Just like Charles, George kept asking peculiar questions and Gina had the answers to meet him every time. "How did the village take the death Mrs Cartridge?" George asks and learnt the whole village was left gutted to the core, when the news of Peter Winselscott's death echoed. He also took away the murders would go down in history, thanks to the way they both happened. It really hit home when everyone he came into contact with along with Gina, when she asks Jeremiah why he didn't fill him in, and it was becoming stranger by the minute.

"Mrs Cartridge I haven't seen George in years,"

"But you are with him now,"

"Why must I keep defending myself? I only came as George's tag along," Jeremiah said.

"Now you have the opportunity Mr Blackworth," Gina pointed out.

To George it seems some tension have been brewing all afternoon between Gina and Jeremiah. This cause him to use another method of Charles, which is to turn the tables on the person they least have as a suspect.

"Jeremiah, do you care to fill me in on the matter and save us these exhausting house visits?"

"I declare George,"

Gina took that as her opportunity to query if George knew the woods where Elizabeth and Peter were killed belongs to his friend. When George looked puzzle she told him Jeremiah's grandfather owned the woods, and hated anyone who trespassed on his property before he too died.

Jeremiah stood and told George he has nothing to hide and doesn't know what Mrs Cartridge is implying. He clarifies to only owing the woods after the reading of his grandfather's will, but it was intrusted to his father until he came of age. Gina would add oil to the fire when she spoke about Jane Winselscott's dead husband, was given a warning to stay away from Jeremiah's land and that he would harm him if he saw him there again.

"I did no such thing," Jeremiah said but stopped from bursting out when he saw it on the table. He barely heard Gina speak about him doing the act, but it only faded in comparison to what his eyes saw.

"I must ask you both to leave," she said

George took her by her words and thanks Mrs Cartridge for her time. He told Jeremiah they are finished here, having the thought of returning but by himself. Jeremiah announced he is happy to do so, clarifying he doesn't want to overstay his welcome. Gina made sure she would have the last word, when she mentions something which didn't go with anything pertaining to the conversation.

"Jane and Conrad Winselscott where very protected of their Peter. I still wonder why?" she said and begins to cry.

George tells Jeremiah to wait for him outside while he stays and comforts Gina. After Jeremiah left Gina quickly asks George to retake his seat, as she wasn't finish talking. He heard an instant confession from her, saying she never really like Mr Blackworth. She passed her observations of Peter to him, as she thought it was wise not to speak in front of his friend. George thought he was well floored from what was told to him, but he couldn't be floored more with what Gina told him next.

"There is something peculiar here Mr Ellsworth,"

"Why Mrs Cartridge,"

"If you wish to enquire, you must speak with the owner of Circus Balloons to find your answers," she said then invites him back should he deserve more information.

George thanks Mrs Cartridge again for her insight, but also words of wisdom. He didn't reveal anything to Jeremiah about what was spoken, but insist Mrs Cartridge doesn't like him at all.

"I swear to you George; I have nothing to hide."

"I believe you Jeremiah." George told as reassurance, then points in the direction they should be heading next.

CHAPTER 13

20TH SEPTEMBER 1960

One of the greatest benefits Mr Symmington acquired on retirement was that of time. He took advantage of his club's lifetime membership, by spending the afternoon just for a bit of relaxation. He sat alone with his favourite drink ginger vodka and soda on ice, and caught up on the interest of today, which happens to be the murder trial of Bentley Wright. To his surprise he read Michael Brimwater's early prediction, that the court will find Mr Wright guilty as charged, despite the strange complexity surrounding the case.

"Can I join you Mr Symmington," he heard and looks from his reading, only to see the god send Peterson Castries standing there in dying need of conversation.

"Help yourself Mr Castries, and to what do I owe the pleasure," Charles said and snap his fingers to alert the waiter, to bring the club's complementary drink, a scotch on the rocks.

From the facial expression on Peterson's face Charles gathered his morning looked pretty grim from the beginning. His accusation was right when Peterson declares today as his worse day known. "The prosecution had a field day on us Charles. Sorry Mr Symmington,"

"Why is that," Charles asks by passing the apology made by Mr Castries.

"Because of the material witness, who claims to have seen Mrs Wright the day before she died," Peterson replied.

Charles tossed the paper aside and open his ears to the only solicitor he has a personnel liking for. He understands the testimony was that of Mary Snodgrass the neighbour and tea companion to Mrs Wright. Mary told the court how Pauline Wright was in high spirits the day before, promising to have tea with her the next day. "By the afternoon of the promise meeting, Mary learnt of Pauline's death. She only accepted the result after she attended the inquest," Peterson told

"She understands the lady died from a broken neck, I just read it in Michael's loathing comment," Charles said

"The court went into chaos after that Charles, the judge quickly adjourned the case until tomorrow," Peterson said

"Did Pauline tell her things weren't adding up? So to speak Peterson," Charles asks

"Come to think of it, she didn't say," Peterson replied and felt how odd it sounds. He embraced the nodding of Mr Symmington's head and this told him Charles's mind is at work. He also thought it would be a thrilling idea to fill in Charles on the rest of the story, but after he finishes the drink he loves so much.

The details from Peterson's court summary, was music to Charles's ears. He took major interest when Mr Castries stated,

Pauline fell down the stairs and Bentley rushed to her aid. He soaks up another piece when the medical report states Mrs Wright might have been pushed, but paused when Peterson had the stare, as if he was about to be hit by a moving tanker truck. He instantly assumes there had to be something peculiar which couldn't be explained.

"Well,"

"Well what Mr Castries," Charles ask

"You see Charles, when I ask the medical examiner under cross examination to states his thoughts on the wound on her feet. He hesitated before saying it was part of the fall," Peterson said

Charles found it quite strange, as usually the medical examiner is on point with their analysis and conclusions. He asks Peterson what his client was doing on the morning of his wife's death, and got another peculiar surprize.

"Odd things around the house, I can't recall. Why do you ask Mr Symmington?"

"You have just tickled my taste bud that's why," Charles replied. He asks another question referring to the address of Mr Wright, taking another sip of his drink.

Peterson thought nothing of it and wrote the address on a napkin, then hands it to Charles. It finally hits him where is the blood hound's second in command and made his own query. Charles told him Mr Ellsworth has gone on a little visit to his friend in Cottondale name Jeremiah Blackworth. If he didn't know better, he would swear Mr Symmington mentioned it for the sake of humour. He caught on quickly when he told Charles, he figures George is trying his hands at being a detective, trying to use what he knows to solve the cold case murders up there. He evens compares the double murders as being by someone who dreamt of being the copycat to jack the ripper.

"Do you dare to explain Mr Castries?"

"To me the murders just don't make any sense," Peterson said not knowing for once Charles agrees with him.

Again Charles allows Peterson to have the reigns of the conversation, as Peterson gave his theory. He points out no one can explain Peter's death which is the oddest thing he ever came to know. This is the reason why Charles has a liking for Peterson Castries. It all has to do with Peterson's thinking ability; you can say it is the common denominator of him and Charles. He brought a real no brainer statement to Charles; by saying the death of Elizabeth Cartridge can be linked to many explanations, which is the difference of the two murders.

"I'm not a detective Mr Symmington, but murders leave their stories behind. Elizabeth left hers, but what did Peter write I wonder," Peterson said and drinks his drink straight up and signals for another one. His second drink came instantly and he made history of it right away. He made an apology to Charles, saying he has to cut their conversation short, due to him having to prepare his closing argument for his client.

"Can I share a joke with you?"

"Go on,"

"I think the jury might just find Bentley insane by dressing his wife up and placing that rosary in her hands," Peterson said laughing then left Charles to himself.

If you thought Charles would have return to his reading, then you don't know him very well. Little did Peterson know the blood hound is thinking on the same line all along. Charles ponders as to why Inspector Stonewall didn't sort other avenues, but then again he might have done that, only to face a dead end. Charles finished his drink and while doing so he took a call from someone he knows. It was what he was waiting on, as it is the opening number for the case.

"Of course George I am honoured to hear from you. I will look into it right away." Charles said then got up and began to sniff around.

CHAPTER 14

3RD JANUARY 1961

Dorielle Stonewall heads upstairs to the master bedroom, where her husband Jonathan lay recovering. At least she was relieved the treatment took swift action in working this time, as the first time she wasn't sure if he would have survived at all. Dorielle enters the room and places the food tray carrying her mother's secret brew of chicken soup, next to him on the bed, then takes up the damp towel and dabbed his forehead, which was rank with perspiration. Jonathan awakens to her movements and the words of "lunch is ready and it is my mother's favourite,"

"I don't feel like it,"

"You must Jonathan, Dr Seawall insists on it," she told before giving a lecture on the importance of him beating this dreadful disease.

Jonathan knew he couldn't win and with all the energy he had, he sits himself up right and allow the feeding to begin. To help him though he spoke on the only thing which has been giving him nightmares quite recently? It wasn't the first time Dorielle heard about these dreams before, but if her husband could get some worth out of it, then she is more than happy to go along with it. "It's the dam murders," he told her pointing they are costing him, some much needed rest.

"It serves you right Jonathan; Dr Seawall prescribed lots of bed rest. You on the other hand keep thinking it is you who will solve the murders," she told. She also points out the matter is in the hands of the police commissioner, and it should be him to do some work for a change, while giving Jonathan another spoonful of the soup.

"Something is not right Dorielle somehow I believe the gossip sisters," he said then coughs.

"Rachel and Lattima would say anything to anyone, who will stop for tea," she replied, then placed the bowl down, to damp his forehead again. While doing so she makes it clear her dislike for the gossip sisters, as they are usually the first to break the silence on delicate matters.

Jonathan raises his hand to block the feeding torture, just to act like Johnny Cochran and defends Rachel and Lattima. He implies it was those ladies who were the first to mention anything about the murders and read the non-surprized look on his wife's face, but carried on anyway.

"Let's hear it Jonathan and I am quite sure Lattima tends to be the helpful one right," She told. She got up only to rest the tray on the night stand, and then resumes her place at the side of the bed, for the story telling.

"One of them claims something was wrong," he began and pulls the covers under his arms. He told it was Rachel who remembered Jeremiah Blackworth during his adolescent years, while attending parties thrown by his parents. He then looks at Dorielle and sensed she is only listening because he wanted her to and presses on anyway. She learnt how Rachel wasn't the nice person she claimed to be as she would often tease Jeremiah about his family's peculiar strangeness when she saw him walking around Cottondale. Dorielle was much too surprized to know Rachel could have a cruel bone in her body but was please to know she could not throw stones at other glass houses.

Jonathan story lingered on and told his wife how one invite to dinner in particular Rachel couldn't contain herself and tease Jonathan when another family member showed similar behaviour to Peter Winselscott, when she and him was alone in the library.

"What so spectacular about that Jonathan, everyone has a strange member in the family,"

"Yes Dorielle but Rachel didn't understand at the time she told me," Jonathan said. He outlines Rachel's encounter when Jonathan's father took her into his study and told her the truth, about the family member who is acting stranger than ever before, this is the reason why they were brought there. "He complained of seeing things and was taken from doctor's care Rachel told me,"

"He,"

"Yes Jeremiah's great uncle Dermont," Jonathan told. He also mentions it was Rachel's last invite to the family's gathering and she was quite happy it happened.

Dorielle thought Jonathan's story was quite funny and even believed that Rachel made the whole thing up. She chuckles then wipes it clean from her face when Jonathan made his next sentence. "Rachel said she found it strange and awkward when he looked at her,"

Jonathan said. He'd watch her use the nursing skills she learnt during the war and prepare his medication, then told how Rachel should have found herself a good husband and stop making stories up about people with supposing strange behaviours.

"I was a nurse you know Jonathan I would know strange behaviour when I see it," she told and gave her husband his medication. She then insists on him getting some good needed rest, not before saying her part which was Rachel's witnessing is due to her fragment imagination. Jonathan thought otherwise and insists that what Rachel told him might have some weight if it wasn't for her busy nosing.

"I actually believe you Jonathan," Dorielle said out loud as she came back to reality thanks to the rain which lashed against her window pane. She rests the book she was reading down and made her way into the kitchen. There she pours herself a glass of water then mutters it is almost time for her afternoon tea to herself, but luck would have it the kettle was right within her reach.

She paused after lighting the stove because she couldn't shift what her woman's intuition was telling her. She made her way back to the chair to await the kettle's sound and while doing so she picks up a picture frame of her husband which displayed a young Jonathan stonewall. She passed her hands over the picture just to shift away the dust that settled, and then reminisced at how dashing he looks in his uniform during his early days as a young police constable.

"I wonder," she said as she stares at the picture but couldn't shake the feeling that had returned, thinking she left it finished in the kitchen. The story came back to her where she then said a name and to her surprize it was the name Jonathan mentioned to her when he first handled the case. She looks through the window to see nothing but colourless drops on the glass. Again it came to her Jonathan's haunting words and Dorielle felt he was onto something when the illness made its presence.

"Could it be, did she really tell you something," she said but cast it off to heads to the kitchen, make her tea with a slice of cake, then return to resume her reading while the rain adds to her comfort.

CHAPTER 15

23rd SEPTEMBER 1960

It's been a year since Charles Symmington entered a courtroom and no one can blame him. His reason is well known by his peers like all the names of the monarchies of England but somehow it felt great to be back. He was treated in the same manner when he entered which would give the impression he is still a presiding lordship, about to sit on some high stakes murder trial.

Casting aside all the above Charles main focus was to get any reliable material before cashing in on the tip Peterson Castries gave him at the club. He took his seat amongst the ordinary spectators to avoid running into one of his associates like Chief Lordship Smart. His plan backfired when he was singled out; but not by anyone he knows, in fact he was a little surprized when Dr Christine Meredith took the seat right next to him.

"Fancy meeting you here," Charles said

"We are both out of place," Christine replied. She even brought into view how strange it must be for Charles to be one among the ordinary folk when he is accustoming walking in from his chambers.

Charles jokily bid to differ by mentioning the trail of Bentley Wright in particular caught his interest, which is the reason he is at the day's proceedings. He took in Christine's smile but paid close attention to what Christine said which was, she always wanted to attend an intense murder trial, so that it could be crossed off her bucket list. To Charles Christine's words was a bit strange but he cast them off to ask her about her brother Donovan when Bentley Wright came waltzing into the courtroom. He was seated like a king in the holding dock on the side, but quickly rose after the announcement of presiding Lordship Nigel Fairmont, who walks in very briskly and sat then ask that the proceedings be carried on in a swift manner.

If you thought Chief Lordship Smart was strict then you and everyone were about to meet his twin brother Lordship Fairmount. He asks Peterson to call his first witness, before telling the prosecutor to cross examine if he so desires. Charles eyes met with Lordship Fairmont head on who didn't bother to care if the king of all Lordships was in his courtroom. Despite that Charles notices off hand Dr Meredith seems to be scribbling something onto a note pad but kept his attention on his own interest Bentley, who looks as though he has aged thirty years since being in prison.

He picked the right day to come to trail as luck would have it Bentley Wright was about to testify in his own defence. Charles wondered what Peterson tactic would be bearing in mind what the prosecution's deadly strike might be, as Peterson would leave Bentley open to cross examination. He also figured Peterson had no choice as Bentley would be the only one to say what truly happen.

Bentley took his place on the witness stand and prepares himself for the first ordeal with his attorney who had everyone except Charles guessing what he will ask his client. They were stunned when Peterson states he has one interest and that was to get his client's side of the story out in the open. Bentley however first stares into his solicitor's eyes then cast a quick glance towards the jury before returning it back to Peterson who was ready to get his show on the road.

"I will ask you one question Mr Wright. Can you give an ideal account as to what happen on the 29th September 1957?" Peterson asks

Bentley focuses his eyes on the wall as he feared intimidation from everyone in the court room. He recounted on the day in particular he was very settled into the work he was doing around the house beginning with the repairs to the balcony. "She I mean Pauline nagged me until I eventually started," Bentley told and paused.

You might be wondering if Bentley was coached by the way how everyone gave into silence and allowed him to speak in great detail. He recalls how all of his tools were scattered all over the floor when his wife came in with something in her hand "The next thing I knew, her sounds where coming from the stairs," Bentley told and listens to the muttering from the crowd.

"Thank you Mr Wright, I have no further questions your Lordship," Peterson said and took his seat.

Charles knew what was coming next. The banks of the Nile river and everyone else were unprepared for the waters prosecutor Biggs was about to bring. He began with the statements from the inquest and the conclusion from the medical examiner who states that Mrs Wright appeared to have been pushed from the top of the stairs. "Did you push your wife down the stairs Mr Wright?"

"Certainly not, she fell I swear it,"

Prosecutor Briggs didn't challenge Bentley's strong proclaim of innocence. Instead he made a little joke about it being sheer nonsense, before bringing into view other cards about the cause of death. He told Bentley and the court how Mrs Wright apparently died from a broken neck, stressing his only fact as to how the dreadful occurrence might have occurred. "If it pleases the court I would like to give a little fact about Mrs Wright," he told

"You may proceed," lordship Fairmount replied.

"Thank you your lordship," Briggs told and with that he retreats to his desk, took up a file then toyed with Bentley asking him if he knows what he carries in his hands. Once Bentley sat silent he continues his damaging rampage by revealing that the file he has in his hand happens to be the medical history of Bentley's wife, which he obtained from the hospital.

The court muttered amongst themselves believing this might be the final nail in Bentley's coffin before the hangman takes over. Charles on the other hand knew too well the dangers of someone's medical history will always rival the cast of doubt against any defence, a solicitor tries to accomplish. He listens as Briggs began firing away without any warning about Pauline's medical condition which might be the cause of her tragic death. "You couldn't live with your wife's illness so you kill her,"

"No, that's not true," Bentley told then looks to lordship Fairmount for a referee's intervention.

"Didn't you Mr Wright push your wife down the stairs, then picks up her body, dress it in her best night attire, then place her rosary into her hands," Prosecutor Briggs hammered on causing the court to become unsettled.

The crowd was thrown in chaos when Peterson waste no time in calling an objection to Prosecutor Briggs outrageous statement. He even highlighted the accusation would have impaired the jury's act of justice and immediately calls for a miss trail. Lordship Fairmount bangs his mallet to command order which came instantly. Once it was obtained he outlined there has never been or would there be a miss trail once he is the presiding lordship on any case. He did however uphold Peterson's claim which is a first for him and told prosecutor Biggs he will not allow such bazar behaviour in his courtroom.

"No further questions your lordship," Briggs told and left to retain his seat then glance over to Peterson who was quite stunned but to let him know his crazy idea has no business being in sight.

To you, prosecutor Briggs should deserve an academy award nomination but to Charles prosecutor Briggs just raised the stakes on Bentley's outcome. He did have some questions in his mind as his eyes meet with Peterson's who couldn't believe he had just thrown his client into the lion's den. "Well given the performance of Claremont Briggs, we all know where this case is heading," Charles heard only to look at Dr Meredith who just smile and began putting up her things to leave. He quickly asked her if she would like to go on one of his appointments but was quickly rejected.

"It wouldn't take long," he insists

"Very well Mr Symmington I will go with you," she replies as both heard the court is in recession until next week, due to the outrageous but thrilling day. She also asked him why? as he usually has his sidekick to do that type of work for him, while he task himself to prepare a theory like none other.

"To the start of it all," Charles told which brings him back to the question he has been thinking right through the proceedings. He escorts Christine out through the court not before asking Peterson another question and got a reply which made him smirk. He led her across the street where they both got into his car and sped off leaving everyone watching to wonder at their own expense.

CHAPTER 16

23ᴿᴰ SEPTEMBER 1960

Like the lost sheep returning to the folk Jean Kalthrough steps off the bus and made her way to the home of her best friend Velda Sweetroum. She knows it had been a long time since they saw each other no wonder she stood frozen just looking at the red brick house and was afraid she might not be recognized. She finally pushes herself towards the door and knocks and was quite relieve when the face of Velda appears wearing a smile on her face.

"Well don't just stand there come right in," Velda told and Jean walks in only to be greeted by the friendly familiar presents of the room. Velda asked her if she is all right, since she appeared to be in a daze of some sort. "Oh, I was just admiring the place," Jean told and came right back to her own self as Velda lead the way into the kitchen where she was about to have her evening's cuppa.

Once the tea tray was place upon the table, both women took the moment to look at each other trying to see if any changes came since they last saw each other. They concluded that the hands of time didn't bother to intervene, and the two started talking, picking up from where they left off from the long talks on the phone on just about anything.

"I didn't do much travels if that is your concern Velda," Jean told and came clean about having a new position.

"Good for you Jean, and I hope the conditions are suitable,"

"Oh they are, I am working for a family friend," Jean told seeing Velda smile which told her she must be happy for her. She watches as Velda remembers how she likes her tea with two lumps of sugar and hands it to her.

Their conversation was mostly about the happy times taking care of Mrs Gwyneth Tallbottom and the conversations she would have with them. If you felt memories was all that was left, then you would be right as Velda quickly jumps from her seat while telling Jean she just remembered she has something for her. She returns with nothing else except a small black box which she hands to Jean who wasn't expecting anything but just the friendly visit.

"I wonder what it could be,"

"I'm wondering the same thing," Velda told pointing out how she made a promise to Mrs Tallbottom to give it to Jean on her next visit to her home. She watches as Jean opens the box while informing her how Mrs Tallbottom left the gift for her in her will which Velda attended of course.

Jean looks at the watch with admiration taking in its design and beautiful detail work which could have only been done by a master designer. She looks at Velda who was amazed by the gift then told where Mrs Tallbottom got the gift from. "It was her grandmother's," Velda told then states it must be Gwyneth's way of saying thank you.

"Oh how beautiful," Jean said

Velda on the other hand didn't want the visit to just be sentimental and spice things up by telling Jean about the visitor, who spoke to her daughter about a week and a half ago. Jean places the watch right back into the box and became intrigued as to who was the friendly guest Velda's daughter encountered. "Please Velda spare none of the details," Jean said smiling.

"It wasn't just one gentleman, they were two. I believed they names were ah Mr George Ellsworth and a Mr Jonathan Blackworth. Stacy said Mr Blackworth wanted to pay a visit also saying he knew her,"

"Well it can only be Mrs Tallbottom as I don't know a Mr Jonathan Blackworth neither a Mr Ellsworth," Jean told and quickly place her tea cup to her lips.

It was odd to Velda but she pressed on anyway by telling Jean why she thinks the two men were over there. She got the fire she needed from Jean who out right quires what it is she has all to herself. Velda went along and claims the two must be private investigators and is probably sleuthing around on some detective business which they figured Gwyneth might have known about. She paused suddenly and was brought back when Jean asks her if something is a matter.

"I wonder Jean could the two gentlemen be enquiring about the murders in Cottondale,"

"I doubt it my guess is that Mrs Tallbottom was one of their school teachers and they came to visit her,"

"No Jean, Mrs Tallbottom wasn't a school teacher she would have stories about it," Velda told. She again notices another strange thing and again kept it to herself.

Jean places the box into her bag after taking another look at the gift she received and told Velda she must be off; otherwise she might miss her train. "Well if what I said is bad news, then I am sorry," Velda told

"No it's nothing like that," Jean told and while finishing her tea she confesses how the murders in Cottondale were a horrible experience for a friend of hers.

Velda agrees and she too resorts back to the time when her son Tommy came home and told her he saw something rather peculiar. "It was on the day I came over to collect the basket and ended up having a long conversation about the death of Elizabeth,"

"What did he see Velda,"

"He saw you crying Jean, after passing you in the kitchen," Velda told

"He didn't he couldn't," Jean denied

"Again I'm sorry Jean I should have thought better," Velda replied

"I must be going thank you for the tea," Jean said then picks up her bag and heads towards the door.

"Will you come for another visit?"

"I will it is just that when you were speaking about the murders, I was thinking about Jane Winselscott. Her son Peter was also murdered. I must get back to my chores," Jean told explaining it was the reason why she became so upset. She then heads down the steps in a rather hastily fashion by passing Tommy on her way down.

Velda didn't say anything in fact she couldn't. She could only understand how Jean feels about losing her friend's son and figured she was very close to the boy. She watches Jean walks down her driveway as if she was about to confront one of the neighbours about something their child might have done.

"I was remembering Jane Winselscott and got back to my chores," Velda recalls but figured the sad news was responsible for Jean's absent mindedness. She thought she heard earlier how Jean had the day off and was pulled from her thinking when Tommy got out of his car after pulling into the driveway just as Jean past him.

"Did you see…,"

"Yes mom it was Ms Kalthrough, how comes she didn't recognize me."

"Don't worry about that, I want to talk to you about something."

CHAPTER 17

23ᴿᴰ MARCH 1959

It was time for the moment of truth; well that's what Jonathan Stonewall thought as he allows his doctor Maximus Seawall to indulge himself in a head to toe examination. The every now and again "Ah huh" sound made by Maximus made Jonathan engulf himself in a sea of anxiety even more, as the sounds didn't have any indication on his current state of health.

"Finish, now join me at my desk when you are finished dress," Dr Seawall spoke and left to await Jonathan's arrival.

"Certainly,"

Before Jonathan could settle himself down in the cosy chair Dr Seawall began giving him the pros and cons of his illness. Jonathan was more than scared in fact he was afraid of wetting himself after the verdict on his life span was given. Maximus gave his conclusion pretty straight forward as he knows there isn't another way of going around it. He told Jonathan there is a little improvement on his pancreatic cancer condition but feared Jonathan's body might not be able to hold out for too long.

"I'm going to die aren't I?"

"To be frank you have less than eighteen months give or take," Dr Seawall replied

Jonathan was more than speechless I bet he wouldn't feel a thing if place in an iron maiden. He sat numb stricken as Dr Seawall wrote up his next appointment and prescription for his next visit then told him to make sure his nurse has it recorded in her books. After Jonathan did what the doctor ordered he filled out his prescription at a nearby pharmacy then took a stroll through the town trying to find some interest of some sort. He passed by a store and managed to see himself in the mirror and could only wonder who that person was looking back at him. He felt as though he couldn't recognize himself from a potato as his once chubby figure has been reduced to a fraction of itself. He watches in stillness as the hands of time seem to be enjoying itself with the charade it is playing with him.

"Inspector Stonewall sir," He heard and turns around only to see newly appointed Detective constable Tommy Browning standing before him.

"Constable I mean detective constable Browning," He replied and the two shook hands for the first time since Jonathan had retired from the force due to his condition.

To ask Jonathan to give the heads up on his illness is the last thing Detective Browning's had on his mind, instead he ask his former boss if he took the vacation to Disneyland as he had always planned. "Why no," Jonathan said informing detective Browning that his time has been bombarded with countless doctor's visits and endless pharmacy trips.

Detective Browning could only sympathize with Jonathan but quickly turns the gloomy get together with some interesting news which might put the sun into his bosom buddy's day. "Say Inspector Stonewall, I was going through you know the other day and that's when I remembered something you said," Browning told.

If you say he shouldn't have, then you are absolutely right. It was Jonathan's worse nightmare, the plague that took everything so to speak, the horror of Cottondale. Jonathan knew it could only be the murders which he blames for his illness, along with sleepless nights and long hours of replaying the interview over in his mind. "Before you begin I must sit down," Jonathan told and the two entered a nearby café where he told Browning he was quite hungry.

They both ordered fish and chips, coke and some water and while waiting for their order to return Detective Browning could sense that Jonathan was quite excited and couldn't hold back his findings any longer. He told Jonathan he was reading the report from the inquest of Elizabeth's murder and found it very interesting.

"Why is that Detective Browning?"

"Well sir it was what stuck out at me,"

Jonathan sat straight and prepared himself to listen when the waitress returned with their orders. Jonathan told Tommy to carry on while he took his lunch time dosage of medication with some ounce of bravery. Detective Browning could only stare in disbelief at the struggle his mentor has to battle and hopes he can overcome the monster which was plaguing Jonathan for about a couple of months now.

"Sir I can tell you another time,"

"Detective Browning,"

"Very well sir," Browning replied and got to the exciting part. "Sir I was reading the testimony of Justine Meadows only to discover something quite strange," he told and went on. He claims the testimony was the complete opposite to everyone else as Justine testimony had to do with the time Elizabeth goes for her Sunday strolls. "Well sir Justine claims to have seen the girl around a quarter to three," Browning told only to see Jonathan in a deep case of thinking. He went on further and told how the time and the girl's demeanour was what Mrs Meadows did indeed figure was quite odd.

"Go on,"

"Well sir, Elizabeth told Mrs Meadows she and her friend promised to meet earlier than usual, as there is some good news she will be happy to tell later," Detective Browning told.

"Do you really expect me to believe that Browning. Her mother stated strongly that her daughter hardly spoke to anyone," Jonathan told

Detective Browning agrees as he was the one to have taken Elizabeth's mother's statement on the night her body was found. He did however insist that Mrs Meadows's statement might indeed have some weight, as it points out at what time the girl was seen last. Again Jonathan begs to differ and told his younger detective the claim only states the girl wanted to do things differently with her follower, whoever he was.

"Sir,"

"Yes Browning."

"Sir the reason why I told you this is because Mrs Meadows is quite certain it was the same time Steven Fairbanks was seen heading towards the woods on the same day,"

Had Jonathan Stonewall missed everything he heard or did his illness had a way of playing with his mind? One thing that is certain is that he clearly remembers the interview with Steven Fairbanks and how the number one suspect at the time forgot to mention this important piece of evidence. It is no wonder the first thoughts of Steven as being the killer stuck out in his mind.

"Sir,"

"Yes Browning,"

"I have to be going, duty calls,"

"Very well Browning," Jonathan said and sat there to process what he just come to understand that cause him to rethink everything for the second time. He let detective Browning go while he stayed back and pondered on what he'd just heard which might be beneficial to him finally knowing the truth.

CHAPTER 18

30TH SEPTEMBER 1960

I might begin a bad habit of bringing in the alleged suspect Steven Fairbanks way down into the story. He is the guy all of Cottondale points to as being the killer of Elizabeth Cartridge and Peter Winselscott. Why he isn't behind prison bars is still everyone's number one question. With his barber cut jet black hair and broad shoulders, the five foot twelve inches' tall young man walks into his mother's kitchen looking for anything to feed his craving hunger appetite. His mother Eleanor was busy preparing one of his favourite dishes shepherd's pie and fired halibut, along with banana bread which will go with a nice glass of lemonade. He applauds her on her choice on dinner which she had been making from the time he was six years old and still is his favourite food to eat.

He washed his hands while Eleanor engages in him in conversation about the day she had. Steven pinches a piece of lettuce and listens to the only entertainment his mother received, as no one in Cottondale talks to her since the murders. "You would never believe who came to my house today,"

"Was it the prime minister?"

"Don't be daft son, the person that came today was Jeremiah Blackworth and a friend of his named George Ellsworth," she told.

Steven nearly choked on a piece of carrot while Eleanor went on like nobody's business. She figures Steven must be asking himself why and told the twist in her story about Mr Blackworth's friend a Mr George Ellsworth who appeared to her to be quite a nosy one. "I'll come straight out and tell yuh, he was asking about the murders he was,"

"Mum what did you tell him?"

"I didn't tell him much if that's what you are wondering," she told

"Mum I hope you told him I didn't commit those murders,"

"I, now Steven, Cottondale got it wrong, all wrong, no wonder they didn't bother to carry on any further inquiries," she told him and went on. Steven listens as his mother gave the heads up to Mr Ellsworth that her son hardly knew the victims despite Peter was five years younger than Steven. "You should have seen Mr Ellsworth's face when I told him we hardly seen Peter at all," Eleanor told and further confess that her son was just eighteen when he went to prison and he hardly knew the girl that died. "He did ask something rather peculiar though,"

"What was that?"

"He asked me if I know the person who owns Circus Balloons,"

"Circus balloons,"

"Yes, but he didn't mention as to who gave him the information,"

Steven could only wonder what type of private investigators there has nowadays, and then stop his mother in her tracks with what he said next. "I have heard of the factory's name before, I heard it from my cellmate while in prison, who used to work there," Steven told. Eleanor turns around and walks with her son's dinner plate, place it right in front of him then sits and begs him to tell her more.

"Well my cell mate told me the young girl was a secretary there," Steven told. He paused only to dive into his plate and reveal his ex-cell mate Marvin's crazy story. Eleanor was counting her lucky blessings as finally she might have something to tell anyone in Cottondale, who tries to insult her while making her errands. She would like it thought to be Gina Cartridge or one of the gossip sisters who have made her life a living hell.

"The way Marvin's story went is like this mum," Steven told while keeping his interest on his own plate. He told Marvin went to his supervisor on an urgent matter, but his supervisor thought it was best for him to speak with the owner of the factory, as he was in his office at the time. "He usually doesn't come around Marvin told me," Steven said and went on. Once Marvin and his supervisor were waiting for the chance to been seen it was there he saw the girl Elizabeth Cartridge.

"Did he instantly fell for her?"

"Not exactly he already knew he wasn't Elizabeth's type," Steven replied. He began to spill the juicy part of the tale by saying how Elizabeth got up and went into the office, leaving the door ajar and it was there Marvin was in time to hear and interesting conversation.

Eleanor felt a thrilling sensation moved through her as Steven states the conversation wasn't among two persons. In fact, it appeared to be between a number of persons where she learnt they were trying to come to terms about something quite important.

"Never Steven,"

"Of course mum," Steven said then enlightens her about the next move Marvin made which was he got up and stated how his legs felt a little cramped and walks over to where the door stood open. "Did he saw anything?" she asked but felt a little disappointed when Marvin was cut off in his quest by the same very Elizabeth, who close the door shut then told him he will have his chance.

"Marvin then told me the conversation escalated very quickly mum, resulting in a woman he never saw before storming out followed by a man, who states it was the right thing to do," he said

The story of Marvin is the right type of information Eleanor could have in her hand. She did however over heard the gossip sisters talking about something similar, with Lattima stating the Blackworth's family might have something to hide. She continues to listen to Steven who finish his story with Marvin been laid off after the factory made some changes with the machinery and him losing his job. He also told how Marvin got into prison which was how he too ended up there.

"You know the papers never mention the owner,"

"Maybe that's why Mrs Cartridge told Mr Ellsworth to do some nosing, maybe she wants to know for herself," he told and the two began laughing.

"Does your friend know by chance Steven?"

"Yes mum Marvin told me who Elizabeth had her keen eyes on,"

"Well let's hear it," Eleanor said and waited like plants anxiously awaiting the arrival of rain.

After finishing his dinner Steven got up, heads to the sink to place the plate down then came to her ears a method Marvin and he learnt while in prison. He whispered into her ears the name of the person then smiles at her before explaining it was the way inmates passed certain messages to one another in order to keep things on a hush level. "One person will tell an inmate during lunch, and then he would past it to his cellmate the rightful person without the prison wardens thinking otherwise,"

"Steven you learnt well, but I never thought it was that person," she said and watches Steven heads off to do his final job, before turning in for the night.

CHAPTER 19

3RD OCTOBER 1960

Whenever you watch a National Geographic documentary on loins, I am quite sure you will come across vultures and sometimes small animals taking advantage of the remaining carcass after a lion kill. It might sound stranger than fiction but this is what our beloved blood hound is getting into, as he looks over the crime scene at the home of Bentley Wright the next day. His invited guest Dr Meredith on the other hand sat and observes his mastery skills becoming more intrigued with him. She might go as far as making him her next case study which would be something to shout about among her peers.

Once Charles became aware he was on his own, he asks Christine to join him on a little exercise. "I rather leave it to the professionals, plus you look rather adorable," she said

Charles smile then pause just as he got to the stairs. Again he asks Christine to join him and to keep the promise she made to him when he came over for dinner. Christine thought he had forgotten but figured it wouldn't be as bad as she thinks. The promise was to continue from where she left off in her personal life, something she hardly ever talks about. She began talking about her first love which was during university while observing how Charles is amusing himself with the area where the murder took place. She stops to ask him if he is getting through because she clearly notices how uninterested Charles became and stood dead in her tracks and watch him.

Charles was at the top of the stairs when he started to look deeply into what Peterson told him and while doing so he began to go through Bentley's version of events. He imagines the tumbling Pauline Wright encountered during her ordeal, while taking greater observation of the floor. He quickly saw the area where Bentley was working on and it became very easy for him to detect the path Mrs Wright had taken.

"Dr Meredith could I borrow you for a moment or two," he said over the balcony. Christine came with much haste and quickly came up the stairs not even enquiring what it is Charles wants her to do.

"Should I continue Mr Symmington?"

"No, not really but could you come from behind that door," Charles said and watch Christine took her place behind the door to awaits her queue. "I'm ready when you are," she said but was told to wait another few seconds.

Charles immediately tore a piece a paper he had in his pocket to impersonate the tools, before scattering them to the floor. He ignores Christine's impatient gestures which he finally gave in and allows her to come out from behind the door. "Charles why on earth you were keeping me so long," she said and was cut short when asks to try it again. At this point Christine was beginning to wonder if Charles is slowly going out of his mind but she was willing to give it one more shot.

"Okay Dr Meredith you can come out now," Charles said and watch her did the same thing as before. "Something is missing Dr Meredith and I might need you to try it again,"

"Mr Symmington I'm not a guinea pig you know,"

"I'm not treating you like one just trust me," Charles replied and quickly rearrange the paper on the floor. He also did something quite new which might go down as one of his methods once it gives him the results he is looking for.

"Dr Christine Meredith I was rather crossed with you on the day you interrupt me at the library,"

"Why Mr Symmington I thought you didn't mind," Christine said and came out and did exactly what Charles was looking for, while holding a pen straight out at him.

To Charles the result surly points in a different direction and this might be the smoking gun everyone missed. Questions starts to arrange themselves in his mind as to why certain procedures wasn't taken into account, no wonder he understood why it all didn't sit well with Peterson. He quickly glances at Dr Meredith and also understood why both the medical examiner and the inquest where inadequate with their results.

He begins to laugh and this caught Christine quite off guard making her wonder if she is about to see the Dr Jekyll come out in Charles. She enquires of course and it was there she learnt what the joke was all about. "You should have seen your face Dr Meredith," Charles told

"You are such a child Mr Symmington," Christine replied with a smile. She wasn't going to let Charles have the ups on her and decided to get the last laugh. She asks him if he remembered saying yes to something when she was telling him about her own history.

"Of course I do, you were asking me to agree on a point of yours, which I did," Charles said

"Not exactly Mr Symmington the truth is you agreed to have dinner with me again tomorrow at seven," Christine replied with an even broader smile

"Well you have won this one; however, I was meaning to ask you something,"

"Of course Charles go on right ahead,"

"By memory could you inform me as to who owns Circus Balloons?"

It was as though Charles became the creature from the great lagoon as he watches Dr Meredith heads down the stairs without a reply to him. He couldn't understand why as he figures it was a logical and simple question to ask. He did however resurface another conversation from before with Christine and it was there he found two important clues, which for sure will come in handy. He came to after Christine shouts to him to say she is ready to leave and while descending the stairs he has in his procession the answer to George's question and why Dr Meredith was in the courtroom. He quickly apologizes to Christine which she accepts and while heading to the car he became closer to the second theory told to him by Inspector Stonewall.

CHAPTER 20

6ᵀᴴ OCTOBER 1960

If the hour of judgement day was just around the corner from Cottondale, you can surly bet George and Jeremiah had picked the perfect time to visit the well-known gossip sisters. They saw the sisters Rachel Rocksoft and Lattima Donahue on the veranda entertaining themselves with tea, cakes and friendly conversations.

"So nice to have you join us Mr Blackworth," Rachel said as she greeted them both at the bottom of the steps.

"It is nice of you," Jeremiah replied but was quickly out shine by George who became Rachel's interest as she turns to him immediately.

"Oh, don't tell me you must be the famous Mr George Ellsworth," Rachel said taking a good look at him from head to toe.

Just like Jeremiah, George said his kind words and follows Rachel who was more than happy to introduce him to her best friend in the whole world Lattima. They both shook hands and greeted each other and Lattima took the time to show how well her historical memory is, by telling George she heard the rumours of him being into town.

However, truth be told she made it her mission to enquire and place herself to see him visiting certain homes around Cottondale.

"I must confess," George replied and took the cup of tea but was left with his own choice of adding milk, sugar or honey. Jeremiah on the other hand quickly mentions he can't stay due to pressing matters which he must attend too, leaving George to weather the storm at the mercy of Cottondale's own newspaper stand.

"Oh well it will just be us three," Lattima joked before asking George what brings him to their neck of the woods.

"I thought you already knew," Jeremiah also joked then quickly bid them good day and left as if not to miss the boat going to China.

"I might have an idea, Mr Ellsworth," Rachel said and laughs.

Again Lattima took the reins of impressment by guessing that George is probably asking around about an unsolved matter, and then takes a sip of her tea and making history of a small square sandwich. She quickly placed the tea cup down to take up a book with a marked page to show Rachel what the obvious thing was, then showed it to George.

"I'm a little taken back by Jeremiah's forgetfulness, as I figured he had told you the details already," Rachel said

"Well I'm glad he didn't" Lattima told as it would give them the honour to fill him in not only about the gossip of Cottondale, but to also show how marvellous they gossip talent really was.

It was like passing the baton in a relay race as Rachel took the baton from Lattima and proceeded with what is sure to be a very interesting tale. She opens up by saying the murder of Elizabeth

Cartridge sounded very peculiar to her from the start and of course George asked her to explain and prepared himself for quite an earful.

"You have to start from the beginning Mr Ellsworth," Lattima said and allow Rachel to again take it from there.

"The Blackworth's was the envied family of Cottondale. Jeremiah's grandparents thought the world of their three children, but after the ending of the grandfather's first marriage,"

"First marriage," George said surprisingly

"Yes Mr Ellsworth, I attended the wedding myself," Rachel told and went on "After the first failed marriage. The grandfather name Cedric Blackworth sent away his first wife with their only child, only to build a nice home in the woods for a distant relative of his Conrad Winselscott and his family, before their tragic lost. Conrad's wife Jane quickly left to return to Cheshire to live with her sister," Rachel told

"Does she still live up there," George asked but was truly impressed with the story so far.

"I'm not sure," Lattima told

"Anyway Mr Ellsworth, after the three children had grown and was married into good families, Cedric Blackworth brought the woods after his son David presented him with his first grandchild. Of course they were other grandchildren, but I distinctly remembered there was another one. I'm still wondering from whom," Rachel told.

George thought it was too much to absorb and can clearly see why these two women are shinned by everyone in Cottondale. In fact, they could be classified as the blackmailers of the time; with the knowledge they know which is spilling out to him like a second language being spoken fluently. He also understands the other two children did well for themselves until the curse made its' debut.

"Curse,"

"Yes thank you Mr Ellsworth, one of the family members started acting very strange and peculiar," Lattima told

George laps up the story like a water buffalo taking a drink by the river bed, after a long journey. It was especially when Lattima told how everyone thought the curse arrived when Cedric made it known to everyone, that if they entered the woods without his permission, they would face prosecution.

"He died a horrible death Mr Ellsworth," Lattima told

"A heart attack followed by an aneurism was the rumour," Rachel replied.

George had to stop them to ask how these stories help with Jeremiah and again got an earful.

"I'm glad you ask that George," Lattima told and it was her turn to tell the story. She enlightens him on an event that took place months after the death of Cedric Blackworth. "A friend of mine visited to say how another member of the family came down with the condition, resulting in the family seeking medical treatment,"

"I was told it was a cousin and he acted in the same way as Jane and Conrad's Peter," Rachel told

"Peter,"

"Yes Mr Ellsworth weren't you listening, I did mention the Winselscott's," Rachel told

"What she is saying Mr Ellsworth it was the reason why Jeremiah's father became quite concerned for your friend's safety. It also stands to reason why Jeremiah lived such a lonely childhood. His father was obsessed with him not adopting the same peculiar action of his other relative, he spent a fortune on doctors and hospital visits," Lattima said.

"The Winselscott's wasn't so lucky and poor Peter was ostracized for his unusual behaviour. He would claim to see strange things," Rachel said

"So what about the murders," George asks

Give your views if you like but it appears George Ellsworth has just secured two new friends besides Jeremiah Blackworth. Little did he know he would receive details which would have him holding the winning stares in a million-dollar poker final game night.

"The murders were more than peculiar Mr Ellsworth; they were the reason why inspector Stonewall had to retire. It led to his illness," Lattima said. She also let it be known it was Peter's death that has everyone baffled. "Mrs Meadows found it odd to have seen Peter and his father taking a walk through the village,"

"I see nothing wrong with that. I do it sometimes," George said

"Yes I agree but it was the only time they did such a thing. They never did it before," Rachel said. She also told that after Peter's death his parents got two unusual visitors.

"Were they family members?"

"Not exactly Mr Ellsworth they were Gina Cartridge and your friend Jeremiah Blackworth," Rachel told.

George never felt so numb in his entire life. Not only was he getting the kitty gritty on Cottondale's two elaborate murders, he was also wondering why the two people he knows would be seen together, when they claim to haven't a liking for each other.

"Oh by the way Mr Ellsworth, you should try talking to Steven Fairbanks, after all it was him who was seen running away when the murder's occurred," Lattima told. She quickly changes the topic after knowing quite well that both she and Rachel had done well on their conversation with George. "I must be heading off to the post office to check up on my allowances,"

"I will join you Lattima, the evening is quite inviting for a walk," Rachel replies. She also took the chance to tell George why she knows so much about the Blackworth's. "I was the friend of Jeremiah's mother Mr Ellsworth, I saw the curse right in front of me," she told. She thanked him for paying them a visit and to tell Jeremiah she hopes his errands were a success, then points in the direction of Steven Fairbank's house to continue on his investigation, hoping to get a thrilling conclusion in the end.

CHAPTER 21

12th AUGUST 1960

Dorothy Twinkleton sat on the bench in the garden with a book entitled "The life story" by Captain Maximus Starlinton as he portrayed his memoirs about life in England's arm forces. She stops to pay attention to Donovan who just sat on the lawn just staring at the trees, with his best friend a glass of water next to him.

"Are you okay Donovan," she asked

"Yes very," he replied smiling then resumes back to what he was doing.

Dorothy tries to carry on but her memory knew better by revisiting what should be the last thing on her mind, the memory of her friend Jane Winselscott.

7TH SEPTEMBER 1955

Inspector Jonathan Stonewall and Sergeant Tommy Browning came knocking at the door along with some company. Jane stood and stared blankly at Conrad crippling away at his hat as if to derivate it into a new fashion sensation. She knew immediately what they were there for and yes just like Elizabeth, Peter Winselscott went missing.

"We've found him Jane," Conrad told her

"Oh dear GOD," she replied giving a quick gasp which turned into a scream of pain and horror.

"I'm sorry Mrs Winselscott, your son has been found dead. Your husband found him in the same place where Elizabeth Cartridge's body was found," Inspector Stonewall told her.

The announcement was too knife piercing to handle. To Jane it would have been more respectable if she would have found out while in a state of unconsciousness. Inspector Stonewall and Sergeant Browning follows the now grieving family into the sitting room, just to get an outlook of Peter Winselscott's autobiography. He only took a brief survey of the room before getting into the part every policeman dreads the most.

"He should be the last person to be found in such a condition,"

"I understand Mrs Winselscott,"

"He was my son, my only child," Conrad said as he leans against the fireplace for support.

Inspector Stonewall asked both parents to give an account leading up to Peter's sad ending, even asking if Steven Fairbanks was any trouble for Peter. He took in how the day began like normal according to the Winselscott's. "Peter didn't have any friends, so he would amaze himself by going to the woods. I mostly went with him, where he would just wonder off but where I could still see him of course," Conrad told

While listening to the briefing Sergeant Browning explores the room and amuses himself by taking up the photos and having a look every now and again. Conrad continues giving clear indication Peter and himself only went to the woods to hunt mostly peasants, as Peter was very fond of his mother's stuff peasant's wrapped in bacon.

"I would make that for him for his tea and prepared soup for Conrad and myself," Jane told

"Mrs Winselscott I know this is a difficult time but there were rumours pertaining to Peter," Sergeant Browning said while still looking at the photos.

"No he wasn't mad. If that's what everyone in Cottondale and you are still thinking. He was just different," Jane told dismissing him from attacking her son's state of mind.

"I wouldn't be surprized if the gossip sisters didn't mention it already Inspector," Conrad told. He also states Peter and his family are in no way are members of the Blackworth's family after Nathaniel Blackworth came down with some unusual conditions, even though Peter showed similar signs.

"I never asked you about the Blackworth's Mr Winselscott," Inspector Stonewall replied.

"I know I was afraid everyone told you otherwise. My mother purchased this land and built this house. So there is no need to harass Jeremiah Blackworth," Conrad told

"It is the furthest thing from my mind Conrad," Inspector Stonewall told.

"Then tell us who would want your son dead Mr Winselscott?" Sergeant Browning asked

Peter's parents look at each other unable to comprehend what sort of question is being asked. Inspector Stonewall backs his colleague by saying it is a pretty logical question and waits with anticipation for an answer. He thought he wasn't about to get nothing but the passing out of carbon dioxide, until Jane broke the silence causing both policemen's mouths to water with excitement.

"Now that I thought of it, Steven Fairbanks might just be such a person,"

"Why Mrs Winselscott,"

"Because," Jane replied and stops to gather herself together then continued "Because he never liked our Peter. He would argue with Conrad whenever Peter would just stare at him," she told.

Finally, Inspector Stonewall had something to link his number one suspect to the murders at last. It was about time as he wanted more than anything which is to show Gina Cartridge who really is responsible. He felt like walking on air after Conrad told him about a particular event, resulting in the falling out between the Winselscott's and the Fairbanks, which also explains what Mrs Meadows saw that faithful afternoon.

"I've kept it to long Inspector, I wish not to open a Pandora's Box, but on the day of Elizabeth's murder, I did see Steven in the woods that day, but he wasn't alone," Conrad told pointing out that Peter and himself went to do they usual hobby.

"Who was he with?"

"I can't remember who but I know he was there. I saw him running away from the woods after the shot that killed Elizabeth was fired," Conrad told.

It was icing on the cake for Inspector Stonewall. How thrilled he was could only be compared to a child at Christmas un-wrapping the gift Santa Claus left him. Conrad continues to spoon feed him by mentioning he took the guts to go and look for the missing Elizabeth and Peter as member's in the village was too afraid to trespass on Jeremiah's property.

"I left Peter there just to do some hunting and when I returned, I didn't see him and figured he went home for supper. When he didn't come home I return to the woods, only to see him there in the same spot as Elizabeth Cartridge," Conrad said and began to cry.

Inspector Stonewall just sat and look at two people become shattered glass portrait by the loss of what brings them joy their child. "I'm sorry for your lost Mr and Mrs Winselscott, Sergeant Browning and myself will see ourselves out," he told them and looks back at Sergeant Browning who nods his head which states they had taken enough time from the grieving family.

As the two walked out and got into the car with Sergeant Browning in the driver's seat. He quickly told Inspector Stonewall about the lovely family photos he was looking at during the investigation. "Those pictures were quite lovely of the Winselscott's I must say. There was one in particular which I found rather odd though," he said.

"Go on,"

"It's' just said family tree, I don't understand it. I pinched it during Conrad's story account," Browning told. He shows Inspector Stonewall the photo who looks at it and also couldn't understand the title either but asked to keep it anyways. Taking another look at the photo Inspector Stonewall saw it was a photo of a young man standing in a well-tailored suit which said something to him. He places the picture into his coat jacket to stay there until he is able to find out who the young gentleman was.

"No time gawking at photos Inspector, we have a murder suspect Steven Fairbanks to consider," Sergeant Browning said as the two heads towards the Fairbanks home.

12th AUGUST 1960

"I'm ready to go inside now,"

"Huh! Sorry Donovan, of course you are," Dorothy said and took Donovan on the inside as a way to stop thinking about her friend.

CHAPTER 22

1ST SEPTEMBER 1956

"Everything is in the car,"

"Thank you Luke," Wanda Chestnut said as she gathers the last two items before calling to her sister Jane, who just sat silently in a chair. She clearly understands why Jane is in this state as her husband and son is no longer on this earth, which makes it easier for her not to stay in Cottondale to relive such memories.

"Everything will be fine love. Luke and I are happy to have you in Cheshire," Wanda told.

"I'll meet you both in the car," Luke told but after Jane asks for a few moments to take one last look at the place she once called home.

Wanda follows Jane as she explores every single room in the house and listening to all the happy stories that came with them. Jane immediately told her a funny story in particular surrounding Peter's toddler's years. "I came into his room only to find all his washable diapers scattered across the floor,"

"Conrad must have been furious,"

"Not at all Wanda, he was helping him along; it was me who was furious," Jane told then went silent then left to take a look at the master bedroom.

"There must be a lot of memories here Jane," Wanda said once she entered the master bedroom. Of course Jane matched her with a story like none other and told it was Conrad and her favourite room in the enter house. "It was in this room where Conrad would twirl me around, while dancing to our favourite song, until we couldn't stand to hear it any longer," Jane said.

She then went to the window and pulls back the curtain only to look at the amazing view she adored. "Come take a look sis," she told and step aside so Wanda can see for herself. Immediately Wanda found the view very inviting as it shows the manor of Jeremiah Blackworth along with his prize winning garden.

"I would sit here for hours and rock Peter until he fell asleep," Jane said

"I agree with you the view is fantastic. I'll bet Conrad enjoyed the woods and both of you visited Mr Blackworth quite often.

"Why yes we did Wanda. During our early years of marriage, we would meet with Jeremiah's grandfather Cedric Blackworth for a game of hunting," Jane replies.

"Oh that reminds me, Luke asks if you are taking Conrad's prize procession with you?" Wanda told

"Let it stay Wanda it only the good memories I'm taking with me," Jane said then released a big sigh before saying she is ready to go, taking up the same very picture that was returned to her by Inspector Stonewall.

As the two were about to head through the door, Jane once again took one last look at the rooms reminiscing on the good old times. She looks at the mantelpiece above the fireplace which carried many a Christmas's past and the visits she received when Peter came into the world. Jane however came back to reality as again she looks at the mantelpiece and rubbing her thumb over the picture she took up from the master bedroom. She then walks up, place the picture on it and began to follow Wanda to door.

"Are you not taking it with you?"

"No need to Wanda. I'm looking forward to a whole new beginning. Have I told you what I saw in yesterday's paper?" Jane told

"No you haven't Jane,"

"Well it is good news. I will tell you after we make a stop to Mr Blackworth's," Jane replies with a change voice full of excitement. She past the rest of her neighbours who only stares at her and can only say "She is probably doing the right thing for the better." She did however looks back and see the home disappearing with history and hopes the person who moved into it would have the same amount of memories as she did. Again her sister asked her if she is okay and again Jane responded she couldn't be better as the car made tracks to Cheshire, leaving everything behind.

CHAPTER 23

8TH OCTOBER 1960

With closing arguments just on the way for the Bentley Wright's murder trial, Charles decided to use the available time to start on his own assignment thanks to the feedback he got from George. His destination is Summer Set House where he is no stranger as it is usually his first stop whenever he has a high class hunch while working on a case. What he has learnt so far along with his gut feeling Charles is certain this trip will be more bountiful as something unexpected might be waiting for him. He makes his way in and heads to the only person that knows his trade Mrs Maude Clementine, a woman around his age, but acts like a sixteen-year-old whenever he is around.

"Glad to see you Mr Symmington. What brings you to my desk," she said and showed more excitement for work now that he was standing right in front of her.

"I wonder if I could have a word with Mr Victor Peetree," he replied and quickly took in her new look and complemented her which she took as a much deserving acknowledgement.

Maude immediately informs him in a high excited manner that his friend Mr Peetree is dreadfully upset over a pressing matter. It appears the new guy David Wiltshire from Richmond forgot to write the dates on four court room marriages last month, so it is left to Mr Peetree to sort the whole matter out.

"It means Mr Symmington the marriages certificates will face at least two weeks' delay before they can be place in the registry," she told and points to David with her eyes.

Charles followed them and saw David who is rather happy doing his work without knowing the trouble he is about to get into. The next thing he heard was the anguish voice of Victor, who appeared to be coming down the corridor with fire coming out of his ears. In order for Charles to get any results, he would need Victor to be on his best behaviour. He immediately thought of a way to get what he wants and save David at the same time. He waited until Victor started yelling for David and quickly intervene by running into Mr Peetree accidently.

"I'm dreadfully sorry" Charles said then pretended to be surprized when the person was Victor. "Glad to see you taking charge old fruit," Charles said and took the book out of Victor's hand and hands it to Maude who just shook her head

"Charles my boy, are you alright?" Victor replied

"Yes I'm fine really," Charles told and took the invitation to join Victor in his office to see if he can cash in on a favour. He looks back at Maude who smiles brightly to his clever trick and had to admit, it saved David some embarrassment. She quickly went over to David's desk and points out what he forgot to do, while Charles get his boss to forget about ever noticing the mistake made.

Victor led Charles into his office where he managed to forget what it was he was going to do. "What brings you here Charles or should I say, whose murder you are trying to solve," Victor said jokily.

Charles wasted no time in getting to the heart of the matter, by enquiring on a name as it relates to murders which happened five years ago. Victor quickly guessed whose murders Charles is referring to as he is very familiar with the obituary which was place in the papers recently.

"I was wondering if the records of Summer Set House can clear a suspicion of mine," Charles said

"I was finishing school around that time Charles, but we should have the records here," Victor told then excused himself to go in search of the book that should have the answer for Charles's question. "I'll just have a pop down by the registry, I shall not be long and I want to hear how your retirement is going," he told and left.

"I'll have the inside scoop ready when you return," Charles replied and wasn't sure if Victor heard him or not. He used the time to reflect on the reason which brought him to Summer Set House in the first place. The reason was the dinner invitation from Dr Meredith which he couldn't refuse. Of course both Christine and himself were back to normal, since she claimed to have behaved rather childish at just a simple matter.

He remembers Christine confessing to knowing Jeremiah Blackworth as being the one who owns circus balloons. It came to that after her father chose to go to Africa with her mother on what would be his mission tour. He got more than he had bargained for that night as Christine also gave her family's life history including finding out she has a relative close by.

"I didn't know they were right under my nose," he remembers her telling him before witnessing the most amazing smile he has ever seen on a woman.

Charles bounce back only to realize he almost had enough to help George construct a logical theory but felt there was still one other thing missing, which leaves his passion for the sinister truth yet to be discovered. His chance came when he took a tour of the home with Christine's permission, while she went to check on Donavan, since Ms Twinkleton is away visiting family members. It was there he concluded the reason why Dr Meredith doesn't have any male followers, as the care for her brother deprives any chance of social life.

He remembers entering Ms Twinkleton's room and instantly notices something peculiar. He continues exploring coming across a very interesting clue before being caught by Dr Meredith herself. "I see your sleuthing got the better of you, Mr Symmington," she said

"I'm sorry I waltz in here by mistake," he replied

"No need to I always wondered about that," she told after Charles asked her a very peculiar question.

"Charles, Charles," he heard bringing him away from his thoughts. He apologized to Victor who return with the answer he has been looking forward to having, as it might just clear a heavy set fog, which has settled over the case.

"I've notice your thoughts were somewhere else but I have the records you are curiously enquiring about," Victor told then places the book right in from of him.

As Charles goes through he keeps his word to Victor by giving the latest news bulletin on his retirement. His adventure started with a two week visit to his daughter and her family. He also told he went to Athens Greece for a little vacation before returning home to good old England. While speaking of his adventure Charles moved his finger frantically until he found the name he was looking for.

"Charles are you trying to solve the Cottondale murders?"

"Yes for a friend of mine," Charles told

"I read about those murders," Victor told then calls Maude and asks her to join him in his office.

Once Maude joins the two gentlemen Victor immediately tested her memory about the name Charles asked him about. "The name does sound familiar," she said then asks to see the book. Maude immediately recognizes the name then took off her spectacles and adds her two cents to the conversation.

"I was a young secretary back then," Maude began then looks at Charles hoping what she is about to say would help him with his theory. Her story centred on a young woman not much older than her at the time. "She was very attractive and came to ask for Mr James Philpot, the gentleman before you Mr Peetree," she told. "From what I observed, it appeared the young lady and Mr Philpot where very good friends,"

Maude's story was the pedestal Charles needed to really get his theory up to part. He understands the young lady asked her friend for an urgent favour, as the normal process of time would be of inconvenience. "She appeared to be in a state of desperation Mr Symmington, I couldn't leave until the matter was solve,"

"I see what you mean Mrs Clementine,"

"There is more Mr Symmington. James agreed to the favour and asked for the birth certificate, where he made his way down to the registry before returning to basked in the smiles of the name you enquire," Maude told then added her own twist. "He did one other thing though,"

"Which was?" Victor asks

"He gave her back the original birth certificate, with the insurance of it been valid if she needs it. The lady asked about the father's name and was told the name was never taken off," Maude said then told how she had kept that secret through her life never once revealing it until now. "I must return to my work," she said

"Thank you Mrs Clementine,"

"Anything for you Mr Symmington," Maude said and walked right out of the office.

"Quite a story," Victor told

"I must agree however something still puzzles me,"

"What is it Charles," Victor asked

Charles told of his concern and was glad to know Victor had an answer for him. "Charles there was another matter much similar to the story Maude mentioned earlier. There was another lady who came asking for Mr Philpot by name, but when she was told he had retired, she asked to speak with me immediately. Maude was on vacation at the time she wouldn't know about it," Victor told.

Charles had to admit that this case had more depth than the story entitled "Twenty thousand legends under the sea." He learnt how

Victor went down stairs to ask one of the other clerks if a lady came to her that he sent down from his office.

"The clerks puzzle face said it all to me,"

"Why is that?" Charles asked

"Two things Charles; first the lady came enquiring about the same procedure,"

"Was it Dr Meredith?"

"No it wasn't, and secondly the lady came from Cheshire, she claims to be a friend of Wanda Chestnut,"

"I see," Charles replied as the wheels of logic began to turn like the 5pm Paddington train to London. He told Victor he finally understands why the murders of Elizabeth Cartridge and Peter Winselscott baffled the police. He didn't give away what he knows but he can surly place the cat among the pigeons.

"There is one thing I must do,"

"What is that Charles?"

"I must re-examine all that I have learnt including the stories I got from Mrs Clementine and you. I must also ask Peterson Castries to see lordship Nigel Fairmount at his utmost urgency,"

"Why Mr Symmington,"

"I'm afraid the jury had already made up their minds," Charles said then gave Victor another reason to testify why he is the greatest Lordship England has ever known. "I must make a stop to a person I over look before my meeting with Peterson Castries and lordship Fairmount."

CHAPTER 24

10ᵀᴴ OCTOBER 1960

The woods should be the last place on earth Jeremiah Blackworth should find himself in, after it has been a place of interest since his best friend came to town. He comes here whenever he gets the chance which would explain his urgent form of exit from George and the gossip sisters gathering. He came to a stop after exploring the same path like a rehearsed routine, stopping at a particular place only to be paralyzed by the memories that brings life there.

A happy thought came to him; no correction, Jeremiah's only reason for coming here was when he faced love straight in the face with no remorse while on this spot. This is why he finds himself journeying to this place many a day. He slowly let his mind take him back to the moment it all began. Never before has Jeremiah been kiss by the angel of love. He thought he missed out when his first wife past away and so locks his heart away until love return to the scene of the crime unexpected, to change all of the above. He was about to go into higher ecstasy when it was all dash away like water drowning a flame.

"Mr Blackworth," he heard and turns around only to be face with another reminder as to why he is here.

"What is it you want Steven Fairbanks,"

"I've come about the offer,"

Jeremiah stared at Steven with much disgust then asked him how he dares trespass upon his property. Steven fired back informing Mr Blackworth that it is time for him to repay the debt that he supposedly owes. "You know how long that I have been keeping the secret? Huh not even the gossip sisters know what I know," Steven said hoping Jeremiah would try and understand his point of view.

"I'm not going to give in. I hardly know you Mr Fairbanks,"

"Someone must pay Mr Blackworth; I almost had to pay with my life,"

Jeremiah knew exactly where Steven was coming from. He paused to rethink his thoughts before clearly saying Inspector Jonathan Stonewall should have done better before the hands of fate took its toll.

"So that's why you and that strange man was seen walking around all over the place. You think you and him could have done better," Steven said

With nothing to reply to Steven's sharp accusation Jeremiah accepts the debate as a lost then asks Steven to please leave him alone. Steven on the other hand couldn't careless, even more push his luck by making another proposal which he is sure to get Jeremiah to come around. Jeremiah didn't answer and this got a little on Steven's nerves which made him show a little disrespect by being informal.

"Jeremiah what say you," Steven asked

"No! It's Mr Blackworth to you. It has been five years you have been asking me the same question. No means no," Jeremiah snaps

"Fine then I will have to fight fire with fire," Steven told

"You do just that," Jeremiah responded then turns around to continue what he started.

Steven wasn't willing to give up so easily and decides to take out the big guns and begins firing like none other. He starts by telling Mr Blackworth he witnessed him on several occasions having word with Conrad Winselscott which was rather strange to him. "Even on the day after Elizabeth died," Steven told

"How dare you," Jeremiah responded but with much anger in his voice.

Steven was less reluctant and matches Jeremiah with the possibility of Conrad speaking to him about his interview with Inspector Stonewall, or it could be about his son's strange behaviour which has everyone in Cottondale avoiding his family. "Rachel Rocksoft told how she saw the same behaviour in a relative of yours. Maybe that's where Peter got his curse from," Steven told.

How could it be, how in the hell could Steven Fairbanks make such a bold move, were just some of the questions which ran through at the speed of light in Jeremiah's mind. He felt like taking the gun he carries for protection and uses it to discard the nuisance known as Steven Fairbanks. He also couldn't believe the petty criminal could come onto his property, only to acts like the new king lion even before challenging the master for territory with wild hear say. Jeremiah however was ready to defend and quickly denied knowing nothing of the sort happened between him and Conrad Winselscott. He even went as far and mocked Steven by insisting that if the rumour is true; it is no concern of his as his taxes already played a part in Steven's joyous time in prison.

"Conrad's son never had any curse and furthermore I never met that man,"

"Not even when you went to his house the day after his son was found dead. The gossip sisters made sure everyone in Cottondale knew,"

Having had the final straw and nothing left to attack Steven with, Jeremiah took out his wallet and pulled a set of paper bills from it. He marches up to Steven and hands him close to seven hundred pounds enough to take him on a paid vacation in Wales. Of course Steven took the money in fact he insults Mr Blackworth by counting it right in front of him.

"See this as the last time you trespass on my land Mr Fairbanks,"

"Don't make any threats to me Mr Blackworth otherwise I will let the strange man know what I know. And one other thing," Steven said and paused. His reason was to ensure that what he was about to say next would stay with Mr Blackworth for as long as he have breath.

"She never loved you," he told then left Jeremiah to sauté in his winning speech.

The words cause Jeremiah to crumble on the inside like a falling building. He closed his eyes for a brief second just to savour the after taste the words left behind. He walks away from Steven and slowly walks back to his favourite place to lick his wounds after the fight. While standing there he looks up to the sky and made a wish to never again he will have to hear Steven Fairbanks says those words again, well at least not to his face. He also found the courage to never allow anyone to see his weakness but somehow he would make Steven Fairbanks see the strength he carries by giving him a stern warning.

"There will be no more from where that came from and the next time I see you on my property, I will be happy to face the hangman's noose understand. Stay away from me Mr Fairbanks, please leave me alone," Jeremiah said with his back still turn to Steven.

Steven began walking away backwards with the biggest grin on his face knowing he had won the fight for now. He turns and began running away leaving Jeremiah to return to his happy moment at the place he loves and holds more dearly than all of his riches combined.

CHAPTER 25

2ND NOVEMBER 1960

Once again Jonathan's pancreatic ailment would have its way with him a prediction Dr Seawall was adamant about. However he wasn't going to let it win all the time as he found the strength when Charles made a surprize visit to his bedside. He immediately welcomes Charles and waste no time in asking his wife Dorielle to bring his visitor anything he wants, well mostly Charles's favourite sandwich and a cup of orange juice. "How are you feeling old chap," Charles ask

"I'm winning by a nose," Jonathan joked then sat up to ask Charles how he is coming along with the case.

"I've stick a pin in it for now Inspector, I have taken the time to come and visit you," Charles told

"So where is George?"

"In Cottondale gathering information," Charles said which should be enough for now. He diverted from the question and took Jonathan back to the moment the two first laid eyes on each other.

"If I remembered correctly it was after you gave your verdict on a case I was the leading detective on," Jonathan said and this made the two laughed. He also told of another encounter which was at a cricket match in Yorkshire where his police team was against a combined eleven made up of judges and lawyers.

"It was there our wives became good friends Charles," Jonathan joked then coughs. Charles immediately lends some assistance but Jonathan flag him away and presses him to tell what he has found out.

Again Charles diverted and continues to speak about the cricket match where Jonathan's team won, then went on to play at the finals on his home turf. "My wife was a lover of the sport," Charles told then stop as the thought might bring back to many happier memories.

"I think that it is time Charles you find yourself another lady friend," Jonathan said and implies it would bring back the colour to his cheeks.

"Well if you must know I have had dinner at the home of Dr Christine Meredith," Charles said and saw a change in Jonathan's face. He asks his friend if he knows the young lady and was surprize when Jonathan told him he remembered seeing Dr Meredith during his investigation.

"I only met her once you know Charles, it was the day after I spoken to the gossip sisters," Jonathan told

"Gossip sisters,"

"Yes Charles, but they aren't sisters actually," Jonathan explain. He was about to get to the juicy part when Dorielle walks in with a bacon and cheese sandwiches and orange juice Charles favourite pig out food. She enquires as to what the two were talking about where

Jonathan held nothing back and told he is about to tell Charles what he learnt from the gossip sisters.

"I thought that was the first thing you said to Mr Symmington, you've been going about them from as long as you have your ailment," she told and sat at the foot of the bed.

Let's go back for a moment. Remember earlier in our story you read Charles and George having a conversation with Jonathan, where Jonathan first gave insight about the case? Well this is the other half of the story, the part Jonathan didn't mention the first time along with everything else.

"What are you saying Jonathan," Charles asks then looks at Jonathan who in turn looks at his wife, as he is about to let something out of the bag.

Dorielle could sense this is something for Charles ears only and excused herself and not that she wanted to hear anything concerning the gossip sisters. In fact, she figures it is about time Jonathan gets his mind clear and finally has some needed peace and relaxation. Once Dorielle was gone Jonathan starts from the beginning. He took Charles on a behind the scenes look of the two murders, which shook England to its core. Again he joked about them having rubbing elbows with the mysterious doings of Jack the ripper.

"I wanted your help Charles but you were giving your intake on your last murder trail the Martin case I recall,"

"Quite true,"

"When the Chief Inspector insist the culprit be found, I was about to turn to you when I learnt you've already retired. I had no choice but to solve the case myself. I did found something out, when I became ill," Jonathan said

"My apologies Jonathan,"

"No need to your wife died around that same time Charles, I can't blame you," Jonathan said and went on.

Charles learnt right there and then all the information and facts about the case, even the tale told to Jonathan by Cottondale's very own gossip duo. He also understood there where many red flags being rose by Jonathan, who found it even more difficult to put anything together.

"The Winselscott's totally fell apart after Peter's death. His mother move to Cheshire to live with her sister after Peter's father Conrad died," Jonathan told.

"Why is that Jonathan?"

"It was when I told her about Steven Fairbanks. It tore her apart I gathered. Believe me Charles when I say none of the evidence pointed to him I swear," Jonathan said. He also revealed the life of Steven Fairbanks and what was so odd about the entire case. "Charles, Detective Tommy Browning deserves all the credit, because when I examined my findings a second time, I thought I was going crazy," he told

"Are you sure Jonathan?" Charles asked

"Yes I'm sure and I remembered where I saw your Dr Meredith, it was the day after we found Peter's body,"

Charles felt as though he had been cast off Mount Everest thanks to what he just came to know. He perfectly understood everything

Jonathan said about the murder, but was beside himself as to how Dr Meredith came into the picture. He won't however press Jonathan any further after Dorielle returns to ask if the two had finish telling each other their secrets and this brought a smile to her face. He excuses himself to make a call to his home in Chalfont St Peter where Chadwick his Valet had already taken out his attire to wear to Bentley Wright's court case tomorrow. He returns to the conversation as Dorielle, Jonathan and himself continues to make the most of the evening, while at the back of his mind Charles continued to piece the case together.

CHAPTER 26

4TH NOVEMBER 1960

"Velda so glad to hear from you," Jean said as both seemed to be talking for almost forever and a day. She asked Velda over the phone about the welfare of her family, where Velda was happy to give an update most pleasing. Velda told how her daughter Stacy seems to be very interested in Troy the boy she has been seeing for quite some time. It appears Tommy has followed in his sister's footsteps after been struck by cupid's arrow with a girl name Kathy Sparling. The news was amazingly superb to Jean's ears especially when Velda also told how Tommy landed a job as the new postman of the village.

"It was Mr Lionel Harman who put in a good word for him, he has retired you know Jean,"

"I'm pleased to hear. Can I come over for tea tomorrow? I'm currently visiting my family,"

"No you can't Jean. Oh it must have slip my mind. I was to tell you the family and I are in London visiting my side of the family. We gathered for the funeral of my aunt Mary who passed away last week,"

Velda said. She also told Jean they won't be back until the weekend and would be more than happy to have her over for tea the following Monday.

Jean felt a little disappointed by what she had just heard, however the colour returns to her cheeks after Velda told she is about to embark on something she always wanted to do, which is to attend a court proceeding right there in London. Jean of course wish she could be there as the thought of sitting to hear how solicitors battle it out for the jury's backing seems like the ultimate thing to witness.

Velda began singing like a canary informing Jean the newspapers has leak out the jury have just reach a verdict on a murder trial. "They are expected to announce they verdict later today. Oh I can't wait Jean,"

Jean reaches for the paper after telling Velda she too came across the article while having her breakfast. She read it out so that Velda could hear again which send thrills up her spine, but came across something very interesting which Velda should be happy to hear. She read Mr Symmington known to everyone as the blood hound wouldn't be giving his intake on the matter, as he is now retired but only found out about the murder trial here recently.

"Jean,"

"Sorry Velda the phone slipped out of my hand just now, you were saying,"

"I was saying I was wondering what happen on our last visit,"

Jean immediately told Velda she could explain the odd occurrences after Tommy stated she walked past him, something which never happened before. Velda felt a sign of relief when Jean mentions it was the anniversary of a cousin of hers who died and how much he loved watches, which is the reason for her behaviour on her last visit. "When I saw the watch in the box, the memories came flooding through," Jean told

"Why didn't you say anything Jean? Oh well I guess everything is alright now,"

"Of course it is Velda that's water under the bridge now,"

"Jean I must cut our conversation short as I must journey to Savile Row and pick up my husband's suit for the funeral,"

"Then if you must we will talk later," Jean told and the two hung up the phone.

Velda found herself hustling to get on her way. She got onto the double decker bus and was quite excited as she never sat in one before. She asked the conductor to show her the famous street known as Savile Row and sit back to enjoy her little scenic tour. She was having lots of fun until her woman's intuition interrupted what would be the highlight of her trip.

"If I didn't know better, wasn't that the day of former Inspector Stonewall's death. I remember seeing it in the papers," she said to herself. It also brought her to think a little deeper as she couldn't explain how forgetful her friend Jean was becoming.

"She never mention it before," she told her self again but quickly blank everything out, so as to not miss out on the site London has to offer and to keep her promise of attending the court to be a witness to the verdict in the murder trial of Bentley Wright.

CHAPTER 27

31st OCTOBER 1960

"I know I haven't seen you around here before, as a matter of fact I didn't know Mr Blackworth had any friends until your visit Mr Ellsworth," Eleanor Fairbanks spoke as she hustles away at making the tea for her unexpected guest. It wouldn't be the first time George heard such a phrase, in fact it was the first thing said to him when he started his investigation. He took his cup of tea and allows it to cool, while he continued to engage Eleanor in conversation.

"If my guess is right, you're probably enquiring about the murders," she said and stop from what she was doing which was making her son supper to have the talk with George.

"Do you have anything to add Ms Fairbanks?"

Eleanor figured by now George had already heard a pitcher full of news about the murders of Cottondale. That's why it was easier for her to say her piece which was somewhat interesting to George. She starts off angrily about everyone in Cottondale thinks and still do about her Steven committing the crimes. "It still get up my nose Mr Ellsworth, I'm not sorry to say," she told. She felt a little embarrass with what she said next hoping as Jeremiah's friend he wouldn't feel offended but said it anyway which brought a smile to George's face.

"I thought Jeremiah was under the covers, you know," she told and laughs at her own words.

"I assure Ms Eleanor it would be the last thing on Jeremiah's mind," George said. it seemed George has a liking for Eleanor Fairbanks as she has one thing in common with the bloodhound. She too likes to be called by her first name, which makes her very interesting to be around. He continues to listens to her and found what she said to be a twist to everything he heard before.

"You see Mr Ellsworth," Eleanor began and went into her own conclusion about Jeremiah. To her he could be considered as a man who lives a double life, one no real man of the soil would find himself doing. George knew what she meant by that which explains her first assumption of his best friend, as he too witnessed the blood hound protected two men in the same circumstance in an another case the two was working on.

"I thought so until Steven came home that afternoon," she told and this really got George's attention.

The words made the tea slip down the wrong side of George's throat making him cough as he was about to finally hear Steven side of the story for the first time. "Are you alright Mr Ellsworth?"

"I'll be fine, please carry on," George replied and listen to Eleanor

"It was before the murders, everything was a lot more peaceful," Eleanor said and continued. From her accounts base on what Steven told her, he would often venture to the woods after finishing his chores for the day. "It was his way of relaxing, as no one wanted to be friends with him. I agree he was wrong for going up there, but it was his only place of comfort, as the house felt like a prison to him," she told.

If George has never heard the truth coming from anybody's mouth it surly came from Eleanor Fairbanks. He wondered if he was feeling what Charles must be feeling when he believes someone is telling the truth right from the heart. He listens as Eleanor states she isn't aware of what mischiefs her son gets into, but he always returns home with a smile on his face. It would be the question only Steven could answer but the conversation took a turn which was much unexpected with what Ms Fairbanks said next.

"Steven said an offer might be reach. He told me we might come into our way," she said and went on "You know he went up every Sunday along with Mr Winselscott and his strange behaviour son, what's his name,"

"Peter," George said while keeping what made him acted strange in the back of his mind.

"Right you are, Peter would do strange things, like acting withdrawn but mostly say he saw things that weren't there," Eleanor said and let it be known how she and Gina Cartridge would talk with their tea dates and try to figure out what was wrong with Peter. She even told about a day in particular when Gina showed her a card which was given to her Elizabeth by an admirer of hers.

"Then it was that, keeping a secret until that horrible tragedy," she told.

It is the most difficult part any case solver has to sit through. George would get first chance as he listens to the turn of events which cause an empire of friendship to collapse with the falling out of Gina Cartridge and Eleanor Fairbanks. "That day my Steven rushed home and immediately locks himself in his room. Frighten for everything is the only way I can put it," Eleanor describe. It was there she learnt but only the next day about the horror that visited Cottondale and stayed ever since. She understands as she told George it was the brave Conrad Winselscott's discovery that alerted the police. "No one knew what happen until Mrs Meadows said her piece, then my Steven was snatch up by Inspector Stonewall and his men," Eleanor told and trying her best to hold back the tears. "I thought he was going back to prison I thought,"

"What did Mrs Meadows say Eleanor?"

"You will have to ask her Mr Ellsworth. As far as I am concern, Gina and everyone despise me ever since," Eleanor told. She even told George what Gina said to her face which hurt the most of all and she never spoken to Gina or anyone since then. "What is it that Gina told you Ms Fairbanks," George ask

"She said they should bury my Steven with his back facing the sky, after they hung him for the shame he has produced," she told

George gave Ms Fairbanks his handkerchief and allows her a minute or two to gather herself together. He didn't have to wait long as Eleanor states she is fine and asked him if he wants another cup of tea. As Eleanor pours the tea a light bulb went off in George's head. He came to understand what the true nature of the case is and yes it was something inspector Stonewall and Sergeant Browning fail to see.

George took himself back to on moment in time, where two pieces of the puzzle came together. His triumph moment was short lived however as the person he wanted to see walks through the door, with the biggest smile on his face and the words which would make anyone rejoice.

"The ship has finally come in mum," Steven said as he showed her the money. He stops his celebration after he noticed her sadness and asks her what seems to be the matter. Steven turns only to see the stranger who walks around with the most hated man in Cottondale and demanded from his mother as to who the gentleman is.

"Meet Mr George Ellsworth Steven. He is the best friend of Mr Jeremiah Blackworth. I was about to tell him what you told me,"

"What mum?"

"About you telling me Mr Blackworth killed the poor girl Elizabeth and the boy Peter Winselscott."

CHAPTER 28

7TH NOVEMBER 1960

The court room was packed as if word had gotten around that Beethoven was hosting a two-day concert with his sympathy orchestra. Charles wasn't going to be left out as he and Dr Meredith sat alongside each other by coincidence. He couldn't help but take notice of the lady who sat to the right of him, whom seemed to be overjoyed by the whole affair. She leans over and starts talking right away about being in a London court room is a dream come true for her, as she always wanted to see what it was like to be present at a famous murder trial.

"I spoke to a friend of mine yesterday about my adventure. It's my first time here in London,"

"Oh really,"

"Yes I'm here for a funeral; I come from a small village and my friend well let's say she moves around. My name is Velda Sweetroum,"

"Charles. Charles Symmington,"

"Nice to meet you Mr Symmington," Velda said before showing some discomfort in the form of playing with her handkerchief.

Charles took the chance to ask her if she is alright but was glad to know she is. He did however learn right there and then that Velda had instantly became worried about a friend of hers who knows someone who have lost both her husband and her son, just around five years ago. He asks Velda her friends name and learnt it was a lady by the name of Jean Kalthrough. He was about to get the story when Dr Meredith interrupted him to say she is surprized at him.

"You do have a way of meeting new friends," she said and only saw a smile came to Charles's face. She did however cast it aside to bring Charles to the real reason why they are there. "I can't wait to see what the jury is going to say about Bentley Wright. I hope he gets life behind bars," she said. Her anticipation rose along with everyone in the courtroom as the jury members began to file in.

"You might just get your wish Dr Meredith," Charles said then asks her about Ms Twinkleton who should be returning from her visit. He barely heard what she said as Velda nudge him only to say what her friend Jean does for a living. "She's a care taker and would the judge be coming out now?" she asked

"Of course," Charles replies

Velda nearly jumps out of her seat when she saw prosecutor Briggs and Peterson Castries for the defence enters having a word before taking their seats on the opposite side of the courtroom. She held unto Charles's arm when he told her the gentleman that just walked in with the two policemen is the accused Bentley wright, who is feeling the weight of the world on his shoulders than ever before. The bailiff asked everyone to rise as he announce lordship Fairmount, where he came in and took his seat then hit his mallet to allow everyone to sit and enjoy the proceedings.

It only hit Velda as lordship Fairmount began to address the court that she is sitting right next to England's most well respected lordship of all time. She looks at him as he listens to lordship Fairmount and couldn't believe the luck which fell into her lap. "I can't believe it is you in person,"

"Sorry,"

"You are him, you are the blood hound aren't you," she told but was hush by Christine who asks the two of them to be quite while she picks up every word which fell from lordship Fairmount's mouth. She also took some notes which she might go over later on and might gave her own conclusion, when she invites Charles to dinner again.

Lordship Fairmount kept everyone on high alert as he continued with his analysis of the case. He knew what everyone else knew about the strong arguments put forth by both the prosecutor Briggs and Peterson Castries, who remains uncertain about the outcome. Lordship Fairmount reminds the court about the events of 21st April 1959 when police rushed to the home of Bentley Wright only to discover his wife Pauline in their martial bed neatly dress with a rosary in her hand and deceased.

"To the police and myself, we found it very awkward and so after a thorough investigation Mr Wright was charge with her demise," he told the court.

The court understands both sides of the law argued for fair justice, which brought them to this moment. Their suspense had surpass the reading of a mystery novel as lordship Fairmount looks to Bentley

Wright and told him that the members of the jury has arrive at a decision, in which sentencing will be given for the crime. He then asks the court to remain composed as the verdict is being read. Finally, he faces the jury and thanks them for their time spent on the case.

"Members of the jury have you reach a decision?"

"Yes your lordship," the jury foreman said as he stood causing both the court and Bentley Wright to have a serious case of butterflies except for Charles.

Charles felt the strong grip of both Dr Meredith and Velda as the suspense was too much to bear. "What say you Mr Foreman?" lordship Fairmount asks

"We find Mr Bentley Wright guilty of murder," the foreman said and heard the gasps and stunned words from the court.

Charles looks at Bentley Wright whose heart sank a thousand times over and who must look forward to a life behind bars. He then looks at Peterson Castries who stared at him and knew instantly he has messed up. He also came to believe what Charles told him at the club would come to past, which was the prediction everyone was saying around town.

"The jury has found you guilty Mr Bentley Wright, however," Charles and everyone in the court room heard. What had everyone baffled was the however spoken by lordship Fairmount, who has never before said the word in all of his years as being a lordship.

Charles looks around the courtroom and absorbs the stunned faces even those of Briggs and Peterson whom are both lost for words. He also looks at Christine who whispered "How can it be," and just sat there in a daze as lordship Fairmount continues to speak as if he had just lost a major football league cup final.

Lordship Fairmount looks at the most sinister mastermind he has ever come across. He knew he would be left with no other choice, but to say what he knows, otherwise Peterson Castries would have an ace in his hand to play, once his appeal for a new trail is successful. He nods his head to Charles as a way to say well played then cast his attention to prosecutor Briggs who just hung his head as he knows his work to get the guilty verdict was all in vain.

"Even though the court has found you guilty Mr Wright, the reason for the however is because a private entity had come forward with newer insight on the matter." Lordship Fairmount told. He also told the court he would not disclose what was discuss in private, but did something quite strange and never before had it be done in a courtroom in England. Lordship Fairmount asked Bentley Wright to state from the dock under oath as it would clear up the only question which no one could answer.

"What was the promise you made to your wife Mr Wright?" lordship Fairmount asked.

Bentley who now regained the feeling of both his mouth and tongue couldn't at first say a word to save his life. He heard lordship Fairmount repeated himself and this time made an effort on behalf of courtesy itself. He began with stuttering words and everyone could understand why. He took the court back to his wedding night where he would have his first taste of marriage bliss, when his wife said something strange to him.

"She said she hadn't finished her vows sir. I asked her why? And it was there she made me promise before I could touch her," Bentley said and continued. "Sir I said yes instantly and it was there Pauline asked me, should she die a horrible death. I must ensure her dignity is intact. So on that faithful day I move her from the bottom of the stairs, dress her and put her to lie down then place the rosary in her hands, as she was a devoted catholic," he said from the docks.

The court couldn't make heads or tails of the explanation except for Charles of course. Again he looks at Dr Meredith who was more puzzle than ever and might just use Bentley's statement as an all-night homework assignment. He then cast his eyes to Velda who felt as though she was at a play in an opera house and then asks her if she would like for him to clarify a few things which she said yes to instantly.

"Well in light with you have said Mr Wright the court sentences you to," lordship Fairmount paused to look at Charles before continuing. "The court sentences you to time served," lordship Fairmount said then hits his mallet and left the courtroom.

No one knew how to react to lordship Fairmount's sentencing. It would surely be a first for the papers as lordship Fairmount is considered to be the harshest lordship England could have brought forth.

"Would you care to join us Dr Meredith?" Charles asked after the sentencing, but outside the courtroom where everyone huddle to express their views.

"No thank you Charles. Why do you have to spoil everything," she said and stormed away.

Charles then turns his attention to Velda and asked her if the two is still on for tea.

"Why yes Mr Symmington," she replies and took his arm and continued from where she left off.

CHAPTER 29

4ᵀᴴ NOVEMBER 1960

Gina found support while sitting on Elizabeth's bed surrounding herself with the treasures of her daughter like a two-year-old at playtime. She held closely to her bosom a little ragdoll that Elizabeth won at the last county fair she attended by knocking over three bottles in a row. She looks at it and for some odd reason it brought Peter Winselscott to mind. Now that she had thought of it, it was the same fair where everyone got a glimpse of Peter as Conrad and Jane made sure he was locked away from sight.

"Have you gone back down memory lane," she heard and turns only to see Roger standing in the door way with his right hand in his pocket.

"Not exactly, I just came here for some piece and quite," she replied.

"What were you thinking of,"

"Would you believe Peter Winselscott?"

To Roger his wife's unusual comment began to make him wonder and was definitely the reason why he sat next to her, as it is the first time his wife had ever mention anything about Peter Winselscott. He hardly settled himself before being asked if he can recall ever seeing Conrad's son at any point in time. "I hardly notice," he responded but agreed with everyone in Cottondale that Peter wasn't in the right state of mind to say it nicely.

"Well the gossip sisters were right about one thing,"

"How so," Gina asked

Roger asked her if she remembers the time she made him rush to the store to buy some ingredients for her famous banana nut bread. "Yes I remembered it clearly," Gina told and came closer to him to hear what details he might have. Roger confessed to actually running into Lattima Donahue at Mr Brown's store on that day. "I remembered telling Lattima I am in a bit of a hurry, but she insists that I have a conversation with her," He told and carried on. He didn't bother to ask her where is her other half and eventually gave into Lattima's demand. Roger went on saying both him and Ms Donahue saw a glimpse of Peter and his father heading down the road and that is what started the conversation. Lattima reveal to Roger how Peter was like the typical child and how his parents adored him. She mentions how the Blackworth's also had a liking for the boy and would invite the Winselscott's to dinner every Sunday.

"Yes that's true I even saw Jeremiah in his younger years playing with the young Peter," Gina added

"Lattima said the same thing," Roger told then reveals a twist that Gina never saw coming. His story with Lattima became quite interesting when Lattima said that after the death of Cedric

Blackworth, Jeremiah's father started to behave rather peculiar after the news surrounding the health condition of one of the family members. "She told it was around that same time Peter himself started to act peculiar and Jeremiah's father told them to stay away from him and his family,"

"Right, it was during his adolescent years that his actions came into question by everyone,"

"That's right darling and that's when they lock him away from air, sea and the world for that matter," Roger told.

Gina took it from there and confesses to seeing the protectiveness Conrad and his wife place around their son. She even told it also brought to what she was thinking moments earlier, about the county fair which was the only time Peter saw the light of day. "To everyone and myself Peter was so withdrawn, that he sat on a bench all alone and it didn't make sense, but he did say something to Elizabeth when she sat next to him,"

"Huh,"

"Yes darling I remember now, I saw them," Gina said. She told that after the fair Elizabeth told her about the crazy conversation she had with Peter. "She told me he said he saw things that weren't there. Elizabeth had a soft spot for him. She told me on our way home," Gina told. It all started to make sense to her even telling Roger how sorry she felt for both Peter and his parents. "It must have been hard on them Roger, I mean his condition," she said

It was an eye opener for Roger who thought he had the best story of the two, but admitted Gina's story had much more weight. He asked her if she told that to Mr Ellsworth but was dumb fumble when she states it didn't appear important at the time. However, he couldn't point the finger at her only, as he forgot to mention something of great detail to her. "You remember those long walks of Elizabeth,"

"Why certainly," Gina responded

"Then I must let you know our daughter had another encounter with Peter," Roger told

Gina was more than lost for words actually she thought the cat had ripped out her tongue on purpose. However, she wasn't going to let her husband kept the secret he knew for quite some time, years to be exact. She asked him to tell her and when he did she was astonished.

Roger felt like kicking himself in the pants for going against what he had promised Elizabeth never to reveal. He betrayed her trust by telling his wife about the time Conrad and his son went to the woods for one of their usual traditions. Once he had Gina's attention where he wants it, he told how she wore the ring on a chain over her neck when Peter stops her on her way to meet her follower. "She said he couldn't take his eyes off of it. She said," Roger said and paused

"Roger," Gina called to him and he took up from where he left off. "Elizabeth said Conrad came up instantly and told her to stay away from his son," Roger told but didn't let up. He allowed Gina to know Elizabeth wanted to know why and asked Conrad to explain his accusation.

"And what did he told her,"

"He told her to just do as he asked then calls Peter who followed him in the direction of their home," Roger told.

CHAPTER 30

12TH NOVEMBER 1960

The two o'clock train from London arrived at Crewe train station in Cheshire right on time. Charles got off the train with some difficulty as his knee was slowly becoming problematic and didn't want to be told to see the doctor again. He cast it aside for the reason of finding a valuable piece of the puzzle, thanks again to what George had reported back to him and his own sniffing around.

He raised his umbrella to catch the attention of his taxi driver who has been waiting for almost three hours. He got in and gave the address to where he is heading as he will meet George who was given instructions to cut his investigation short to join him before moving on any further. He spotted George waiting for him and stops the taxi to let him in and continued on his way. "I hope you took Cottondale by storm George," he joked

"Never in my life have I taken in so much. How do you do it Charles," George replies. He even brags to Charles about finding the perfect rival for The Edge newspaper, pertaining to the gossip sisters.

Charles smile but kept what he is about to discover hidden, and wouldn't mind teaching George as it would be the perfect example altogether. Along the way both Charles and George shared their findings then turns the topic into something pretty unexpected. "I feel there is more to what I am hearing Charles,"

"Why is that," Charles replies.

"I can't really explain but I know it is there,"

Charles then asks him if he spoken to Jeremiah as in getting his side of the story but to his surprize George had already thrown out any accusation which might points at his friend. He even declared he will never believe what anyone might say if it turns out Jeremiah might be the one responsible for the crimes. Charles shook his head as he knows George is very insecure about his findings, despite there are rather strong clues to latterly construct a possible theory. However, he hopes with what he is about to discover it might change everything they learnt so far.

They arrive at their stop which was right in front of a lovely English style cottage complete with a well-manicured lawn. Charles got out and quickly surveyed the surroundings before turning to tip the driver along with waiting for him when he returns. "Very well governor," the driver said and quickly pulls up the brakes and snuggle himself hoping to catch a little snooze before his client return.

Charles and George approach the house and knocks on the door which was quickly answered by a very attractive young woman. George nearly forgot his manners and quickly spoke to her but allowed his well charmed buddy to do all the talking.

"I'm sorry gentlemen but you have the wrong house. Mrs Chestnut is two houses down," she said and points to another well maintain home with an almost similar manicured garden just like the lady's. Charles made small talk and asked the young lady a peculiar question, where he was wondering if the lady by chance if she saw visitors at Mrs Chestnut's residence.

"I'm not sure. No wait a minute, I only saw one visitor and I believe it is her sister. She comes on regular bases," the lady told where Charles thanks her for her co-operation.

They past the same taxi driver and heads to the home with a beautiful flower garden but with a yellow brick walk path much similar to that in the Wizard of OZ. Charles again took the lead and knocks on the door which was open by a middle age lady with a nice personality. "Good afternoon Mrs Chestnut,"

"Good afternoon yourself and May I ask who are you," she replied

Charles puts his blood hound's cleverness to good news, by telling Mrs Chestnut he is house hunting and wanted to know if she is interested in selling her home to him for a substantial among. Mrs Chestnut immediately declines the offer as she is quite content with her home and wouldn't give it up for anything. She did however invite them in as she reveals she is trying to get her sister to sell her house for quite some time.

"May we have a word with her?" Charles asks

"Of course you may I will fetch her for you," she told

They followed her into the sitting room where Charles quickly asked to see the newspaper only to read what the weather forecast might be for tomorrow. "I'll get it for you and by the way you can call me Wanda," she told then calls to her sister to join her as they have invited guest.

"My name is Charles and this is George," Charles said and took the paper then sat and started to read with it up close and personal to his face.

As Charles search for the weather forecast it was up to Wanda and George to make small talk. George commented Wanda on the décor of her home but was surprized when she states it is the work of her husband who is a carpenter by trade. "When we brought this house, it was in great need of repair," she told jokily

Charles said from behind the paper about him wanting to purchase a new home as he getting tired of the one he has and the same old view. George played along saying how his friend is constantly nagging him about finding a new home where he can and his wife can spend more time together.

"I'm certain my sister's home in Cottondale would be more suitable," Wanda told and again shouted for her sister to come and join her and the guest.

"Oh yes I have seen the house you are referring to Mrs Chestnut, as I visited up there recently," George replied and took a sip of his tea.

Wanda was impressed with what George said and made joked that he might know her sister who came from around that area. She was about to give him a little history when her sister walks in and apologize for her late absence. "Jane I mean Jean I invited these two gentlemen after they offered to buy my house, but I told them about yours instead," Wanda replied. She also told of George's recent visit to Cottondale saying that he was visiting a long-time friend of his and might have seen her around. She also apologized for calling her sister by another name, as she gets quite confused with them both.

"I'm quite sure I haven't seen him before," Jean told and lost her footing after Wanda points to Charles as being the person who is indeed interested in buying her house.

Both men quickly lend assistance to her, where she took rest right next to her sister. Wanda gives her a cup of tea to revive her while asking if she doesn't feel well. "I'm dreadfully sorry gentlemen it's never happen before," Wanda told

"I'm fine Wanda I just lost my balance that's all," Jean replied

"It must be my aftershave," Charles said jokily then change the topic by mentioning he had just come from the court after the reading of the verdict in the trial of Bentley Wright. He mentions about running into a lady friend of his who he invited to lunch where they both gave their views on the outcome of the case.

"I too was rather surprise when I read it in the papers," George told

"I as well, I thought he was going to spend the rest of his life in jail," Wanda told then looks at Jean. "Your friend Velda went to London recently Jean, do you remember,"

"Yes I do but I don't remember her telling me she met someone," Jean replied

"I believe he was found guilty I think, but the judge did something quite unexpected," Wanda told

"From what I gathered the man was found guilty but was given time served," Charles said then returns the topic back to his main matter of interest. George agreed and asks Charles if he made up his mind about wanting to buy the house in Cottondale.

"I'll stick a pin into it for now," Charles said then stretches out his leg as his knee waited for the perfect time to act up.

Wanda became very interested in how Charles's knee is giving him much trouble, where Charles was happy to tell her a little history. He said he feel off his bicycle and hit it against the pavement just the other day. He claims it only happened recently and should be fine in a day or two. He jokes about his mishap as being the history lesson for the day, and then asked Jean if she doesn't mind giving a go at it.

"Do you mean cycling?"

No Jane, sorry Jean, I mean tell me and George a little about yourself, as I am into life stories and all that," Charles said

Jean looks at Wanda who says she doesn't see anything wrong with his query and was happy to oblige. She starts off as being the adventurous one in the family where she travelled a lot during her earlier years before returning home to Cheshire to be with her family. She quickly remembers and told she was never the one to be struck by loves arrow, that's why she never visited the churches alter.

"I see, but you have a ring on your finger," Charles pointed out and she quickly looks at her left hand. "Oh I forgot about that. I did accept a marriage proposal once, but I cancelled it and kept the ring," Jean said

"I remembered it as well. You did say he wasn't your type right Jane, sorry Jean," Wanda said to back up her sister's story.

"That's true Wanda,"

"I see," Charles told then looks at the clock only to realize how time was slipping away and quite fast. He turns to George and told they must be going, as both have overstayed their welcome. George quickly looks at his watch so to do Jean, as they heard Charles states he might still be interested in buying the home in Cottondale.

"I will think about it Charles,"

"Get back to me as soon as possible," Charles said and gave her a piece of paper with his number on it. He notices the watch she wore on her hand and became very interested in it as well. He told his wife would like to buy one of the watches for a friend of hers and ask Jean where she brought it.

"It was a gift from a friend," Jean said and touches the face of the watch very softly with her hand.

"Well asked your friend to give me a call as to where I can buy one from," Charles said giving Jean his number.

"Well do," Jean said then told she needs to lie down to rest her head from the mishap she had encountered earlier on.

As the train was heading back to London Charles sat alone with his thoughts to go through what he heard and learnt so far. He had to admit to George about being right about the investigation so far then asked George if he is still going to have word with Jeremiah.

"I will not Charles, I have already ruled him out," George told

"I see, but I think we both need to return to Cottondale George,"

"Why Charles,"

"Because I believe we still don't have all the information," Charles said as he knows there is one person who might have the answer he is looking for. He knew the one person whose story can shed the light he is looking for and has been with the puzzle pieces all along, the story of Mrs Justine Meadows.

CHAPTER 31

31ST OCTOBER 1960

The dreaded telephone painted it all to Dr Maximus Seawall as he rushes to the home of the Stonewall's. It would be foolish of me not to say want was on his mind but he hopes for once to be wrong as so far his predictions on Jonathan's illness has pulled right through from the start. He enters barely taking notice of Dorielle who sits next to her husband wrapped in a blanket of despair but with hope Jonathan will pull through just like before. She even went as far as to have his favourite shirt ready in her lap just in case it was a false alarm.

"Any progress before I came Mrs stonewall?"

"No Dr Seawall. I tried just about everything," she replied

Maximus could see her efforts as he had known her to be the best village nurse Cottondale could ever imagine having. As a matter of fact, he is quite sure she applied all her nurse's skills, which led to him being her last and only option. What struck at him the most was when he saw her rested her hand on Jonathan's forehead and he knew right there he had to make every minute count if Jonathan is to make it out alive.

Like all general practitioner's Dr Seawall did his usual routine of an examination then asked why Jonathan didn't option to go to the hospital. Dorielle came up with the excuse of her husband was too weak which is why she called him at short notice. To be fair Jonathan was indeed weak, he couldn't even move to save humanity and it was evident to Dr Seawall who confirms it. He taps Jonathan to keep him in tune with him, while he works tirelessly around the clock to beat death at its own game.

"Jonathan, Jonathan" he calls again but this time he thought Jonathan was having another symptom he wasn't sure about. For Jonathan began to mutter words which didn't made any since to him at all, words which would need a translator to translate. He put his ears a little closer to Jonathan's lips and could barely make out what he was saying.

"It all makes sense now, I finally know the truth," Jonathan's quivering lips whispered as he held onto Dr Seawall.

"For Christ sake Jonathan stay with me," It was the only message Dr Seawall's mind could come of with. He didn't care what Jonathan was trying to tell him, it was not his place so to speak. He stops Dorielle from coming closer as his ego got the better of him. Everything was on the line from this moment onwards to Dr Seawall this meant the worth of his career. As he fights he listens to Dorielle as she gives her award winning speech. She speaks to Jonathan reminding him about their lives together, beginning with the love at first sight moment. "It was at Commissioner Stanton's retirement function," she began. Her story should be the pedestal valentine's days stood on as it reflected what love truly holds dear. They met that night after Dorielle went with her then boyfriend, but give it up at the start, once she laid eyes on Jonathan.

"Then came Darrell, Jonathan he is on his way here Dr stonewall," she told

"Dorielle I love you, but they did it so well," Jonathan whispered to her but it appeared she didn't hear him, as she was much too busy saying how being the wife of a police constable is her life's work. "I wouldn't trade it for anything," she said as her female intuition told her she might have to carry on without him.

From Dr Seawall's observation the fate of Jonathan hung in the balance. His vital signs were of major concern, while his heart beat calls for all hands on deck, as it approaches a storm like none other. His fear soon became a reality when he Jonathan looks into his eyes then blinks to say it is all over. Death has won; it never plays fair and is the only winner in these types of situations. Again he lent his ear to Jonathan's lips once again only to hear his final words and listens with great precision.

Downstairs the front door flew open where a couple dash through like a stampede of wildebeest. They left everything by the front door and rush upstairs only to stop when they approach the open door facing them and were prepared to face the music.

"Darrell and Alice," they heard and ran into the arms of Dorielle who couldn't hold back.

"Am I too late?" Darrell asks as he felt his mother's warm but tight embrace.

"Mrs Stonewall it will be alright," Alice told as she completes the circle of three.

"Time of death 7:15 pm. I'm sorry there is nothing more I can do," Dr Stonewall said as he began packing his doctor's bag. He came straight out and told he would have to fill out Jonathan's death certificate, then throw the grieving escapade right off course.

Dorielle turns and faced him then looks at Darrell wondering what on earth could be left behind as death usually takes everything like a debt collector. Was Dr Seawall ready? I doubt it but he knew the last words of any deceased must be honoured no matter what the cost.

"It doesn't matter doctor, my father is dead," Darrell spoke with the dark shadow of grief looming high about.

"Yes it does matter. It matters to me what did he say," Dorielle said also saying the last words spoken by someone represents the closure of one's existence.

"Very well Mrs Stonewall," Dr Seawall said and paused just to gather himself together. "His last words were I love you Dorielle and,"

"And what Dr Stonewall," Alice replied waiting with panted breath for the final result.

Dr Seawall looks at Dorielle and hopes she doesn't go crazy on him as he mustn't keep them in suspense any longer. "He also said to ask her. Those were Mr Stonewall's last words," he told.

Of course the first part made perfect sense but neither Dr Seawall nor the others could comprehend with the last part of the sentence. Dorielle immediately confess that her husband was always the one to play tricks on the mind with his silly phrases. She repeats the sentence to herself again and just like the light bulb she knew want exactly Jonathan was referring to.

"He knew,"

"What mother?" Darrell asks then looks at his girlfriend who wishes someone would just bring her up to speed and fast.

"He knew who the killer is," she said then asked Dr Seawall if her husband mention a particular name.

"Why yes Mrs Stonewall, Jonathan asked that his words be spoken to the blood hound, a Mr Symmington," Dr Seawall said then told he must leave as he has Jonathan's paper work to fill out and will make the call to the police and corners downstairs. "I'm sorry for your lost," he told and left without giving any thought as to who Jonathan was referring too.

Once he was gone Dorielle walks up to the bed, picks up the sheet and covers the image that was once her pride and joy.

"Mother what are we going to do," Darrell asks

"We are going to prepare Jonathan for his funeral, then honour his last words. That's what we are going to do," she said while knowing that her husband finally caught the killer, no wonder he was happy to die.

CHAPTER 32

11TH NOVEMBER 1960

Dr Meredith sat at her desk going through some research information she had just gathered on schizophrenia. If lucky it will help her find the cure she is looking for and make a giant step for internal medicine. So far the information she gathered is yielding some well deserve results which might be the bases for her book which she plans on publishing next year.

Somehow Christine found there was still some questions which need to be answered about such human behaviour and this led her to recall the conversation she had with Charles at the library. She ponders as to why Charles also had an interest in that sort of behaviour without giving any real reason for his study. "I wonder if it has to do with the Bentley Wright case," she said to herself and resorted back to her papers only to come across the notes she gathered from attending Bentley's murder trial.

While reading she realize how evident her notes where that she got up and retrieved a file of hers, which she kept from the moment the case was given to her. The file contains the observations of a former patient of hers who showed similar behaviour to that of schizophrenia. She places the pen down and recalls the testimony of Bentley Wright and had to believe there was some truth to what he was saying.

"I guess it started in her earlier years," Christine recalls Bentley saying those words on the witness stand.

She tries to continue on but the hurdling thoughts kept coming like a train at full speed and this made her more inquisitive than anything else. The first thing came to mind was why Mr Symmington didn't react stunned like everyone else during the reading of the verdict. After all lordship Fairmount is known for giving sentences no less than thirty years to eternity once an accused is found guilty of murder. Another question which stood out in her mind was how lordship Fairmount would be seen among his peers from now onwards. "I wonder if Charles had something to do with it all?" Christine asked herself, while having the fear that the blood hound probably had some conniving scheme cooked up and served it cold.

Things got really interesting for her when she took herself back to the night she invited Charles to dinner. The highlight of the evening was to get Charles out of his comfort zone and probably engage in some other type of interaction. However, it placed second to the interest Charles had in Donovan's peculiar behaviour and how much he knew about it which was a bitter sweet moment to her.

"You are peculiar Charles but rather handsome," Christine said smiling

She eventually managed to drop down her conclusions but again hit the curve when it all stood right in front of her as if seeing a miracle from God in full bloom. "How dare you Charles," she said as it became apparent as to why Charles was unmoved during the verdict's reading. "You knew what happen Charles, that's what you, hung over lordship Fairmount's head," Christine said while feeling a knife pricing stab to the heart.

A sudden fear crept over her where she remembers Charles mentioning he has to visit a friend of his in Cottondale. She felt as though the walls were closing in on her as the fear became more visible than ever. You are to guess what the fear is which is your homework assignment due before the end of the story.

Christine began packing as if trying to escape from an abusive marriage and catch the next train before the next sixty seconds past. Why? It is a must to her, in fact its life or death at this point. She made the mad dash to the professor's lounge and quickly dials for the operator. "Yes give me line 6472," she said and waited madly for an answer which came through at the first ring.

"I've being trying to get hold of you Dr Meredith,"

"I understand Ms Twinkleton but I must ask you a very important question," Christine said

"Yes Dr Meredith,"

"Have you received a visit from Mr Symmington," Christine asked. She nearly lost all sense of composer as it became clear to her, when she allowed the blood hound to take a tour of her home, a mistake she will gladly take with her to the grave.

"Dr Meredith,"

"I'm here, sorry Dorothy," she said

"Mr Symmington didn't paid a visit today,"

"Good I'm glad to hear that," Christine said as she could only imagine what else the blood hound already knows.

CHAPTER 33

5TH NOVEMBER 1960

The light sprinkle of rain was indeed the perfect weather for the bereavement of Jonathan Stonewall. George could only absorb the motionless nature adapted by Charles as he watches the casket allowed the earth to swallow it whole like a python consuming its prey. It made him look at the friendship he has with Jeremiah in more detail and came to a conclusion with the ultimate question in mind, which was has Jeremiah been truthful all along? He lends over to Charles and asked him if he would like to return to the church to gather himself together, knowing Charles has just begun to recover thanks to his trauma some months ago.

"I will take you up on your offer George. I will meet you back at Jeremiah's manor," Charles said

"Very well," George replied and watched his only true friend became invisible as he excuses himself from the proceedings to seek sanctuary in the church.

"Is he alright," Jeremiah asked

"If I know Charles as well as I do, he will be back to himself before the last sprinkle of dirt rest upon the grave," George told

Father Thomas Whitebrook looks at Dorielle before ending off his bible lesson. He closes the ceremony with the phrase "Ashes to ashes, dust to dust," then made the sign of the cross with his hands, then gave way for the mourners to bit their final farewell. Dorielle took her queue and proceed to have her final words to her husband by dropping a single rose onto the casket. She then returns to her son and buries her face in his jacket to help her cop with her goodbyes.

"Everything will be alright mother," he told her as he still struggles with the death of his father.

"I know it will Darrell," she replies then took her face from his jacket when she heard Inspector Browning spoke for the first time since Jonathan's death.

"I'm sorry for your lost Mrs Stonewall. Your husband will be greatly missed," he said

Dorielle couldn't respond at first instead she walks up to him and brush her palm against his cheek then nods her head as an agreement. She was glad it was all over as she has one other thing on her agenda, which is to speak with the person who cared for her husband just as much as she did. "Where is he George?"

"He is in the church,"

"Thank you and Darrell I will meet you and Alice back at home," she said and made her way to find the blood hound.

Dorielle walks in only to see Charles sitting alone just staring at the cross with the image of Jesus attach to it. She took careful steps not to disturb him, then quietly sat next to him and stared at the crucifix. Charles broke the silence by apologizing for him walking away from the casket, but was quickly silence when Dorielle rest her hand on his arm.

"My husband was your biggest fan Charles. He would talk for hours about your proceedings in court and never grew tired," she said smiling

"I was one of his," Charles replies. He describes how Jonathan was the ideal policeman turn Detective and it is going to be impossible for anyone to fill his shoes. His words were a badge of merit to Jonathan's legacy which was music to Dorielle's ears, however he paused when she gave the reason for her joining him.

"The truth is Charles I'm not here to talk about Jonathan's burial. I'm here to tell you Jonathan's clue to the case," she said

Finally, someone has caught Charles off guard and Dorielle was having the honour of it all. She embraces his curious stare then taps him on the arm and surprized him for the second time. "I have the rest of my life to grieve, but I must insist on carrying out the duty of my husband," she said and started from the beginning.

She reveals she already knew Jonathan came to him for help about the two murders and points him in the right direction. "I had to agree with him it did seem odd at the time and that was what kept Jonathan interested I must say," she told.

Charles learnt how Jonathan would still pick at the case changing his theory every now and again during his illness. She lets him in on a conversation her husband had with Detective Browning and what he learnt about a peculiar observation by one of the villagers. "Justine

Meadows said the time was wrong. She claims to have seen the girl earlier that day Charles,"

"I see. Did Mrs Meadows say where the girl was heading?" Charles asked

"No she didn't, however she did say the girl was off to meet a friend, since they had made earlier plans during the week," Dorielle said then tried desperately to hold back the tears.

Charles gave her his handkerchief then wraps his arm around Dorielle's shoulder and could barely understand what she was saying. He manages to get her to repeat and became her support when she told him about the friendship him and her husband had which is why she must do her part and let him know what it is Jonathan was so happy to die for. "He loved it all Charles, which brings me to the best part," she told and resumes her composer, while playing with the handkerchief.

It was like being in a torture room as Charles could only wonder what it is Dorielle is holding back. He already got the bulk of it all which will give him more than cherished memories and listens as Dorielle rein act the last day she spent with her husband. She reveals the truth about Jonathan not wanting to go to the hospital which was the reason why Dr Seawall was summoned.

"Jonathan always told me if anyone should die, it should be around family. So I called our son Darrell on the last day you came to visit. Do you remember Charles?"

"Of course I remember, it was there I learnt about the gossip sisters," Charles replied

Dorielle smiled through her grief then continued on about Darrell boarding the first train back home and was in time to see his father leaving the earth. She also told it was on that day she learnt what Jonathan had been spending his life trying to solve. "They were very peculiar words they were. I still can't make any sense out of them,"

Charles completely turns and faced Mrs Stonewall. He was so infatuated with what she might say, that he forgot he was grieving over the death of one of his closest friends. "What is it he said Mrs Stonewall,"

"Well the first part I understood quite clearly," she said before drying her eyes once again. "Charles, he said to ask her. Don't you find it bazar for him to say such a thing," she replied

"Not I don't Mrs Stonewall," Charles told as Jonathan's words were what was needed to place Charles at the center of the unfolding mystery. He stood up immediately and gave his arm to Dorielle who didn't hesitate for a moment; despite she didn't know what got into him.

"I don't understand Charles,"

"No need to Mrs Stonewall, because your husband did me one last favour," Charles said as he escorts her out of the church to join Darrell and the others on celebrating the life of his friend Jonathan Stonewall.

CHAPTER 34

5TH DECEMBER 1960

"Why Jean it's been quite a long since you've called," Velda said while entertaining herself with the decoration of the Christmas tree. She was overjoyed to hear from Jean on the exact day Mrs Gertrude Tallbottom died one year ago.

"I was rather busy," Jean replied and also claim to be in the festive spirit but truth be told she haven't got around to anything which resembles Christmas at all. She did however confess as to why she called, which is to discuss something surrounding Mrs Tallbottom.

Velda wonders why her friend is so interested in the decease old lady but went along anyway with the conversation. They both agreed about the year's anniversary of Gertrude's death and remembered like it was yesterday, but Jean wanted to know something in particular and asked Velda if Mrs Tallbottom said something to her after she left.

"Well the last thing I remembered Jean is Gertrude speaking about the inheritance of Jeremiah's father. It was about some business I gather," Velda told. She did however give the bulk of it all and told Mrs Tallbottom found it very peculiar when a Dr Meredith's father was supposed to take over, from a cousin who had to seek medical attention. "I hope it helps Jean," Velda told

"Are you sure she didn't say anything else,"

"Quite. No wait, she did say Inspector Stonewall was enquiring the whereabouts of a Jane Winselscott,"

"I'm sorry the phone slipped out of my hand," Jean told then gave her own insight as to why the police are searching for a friend of hers. She explains how Inspector Stonewall probably wanted to know how Jane Winselscott is coping with life, after the death of her son and all.

Jean looks away at a small picture of a little boy which her friend Jane gave to her. She instantly remembers the happy stories of Jane and her Peter never feeling so alive in all her life. It all change however when Jane told her about her son's tragic death, which was a catastrophic blow to her happiness making it hard for Jean to hold anything together.

"Are you there Jean," Velda asked after hearing nothing else but silence.

"Yes I'm here but I will have to call you back," Jean said and hung up the phone.

She watched the picture which took her back to the headlines that graced the papers all over England. The papers stated how another body has been found and the strange occurrence that came with it. The body had been found in the exact same place as the body of the first victim some two weeks earlier. One editor dubbed the murders as horrific, while another described the killer as a horrible beast and should be sent straight to hell first class. It was the first time anything so gruesome had happen in Cottondale, no make that England on the whole.

For some reason Jean thought she was Jane as she made the trip by taxi to the house that Jane once lived in. She climbs the steps then turns to the once manicured lawn complete with flower garden and could only agree, that was Jane's favourite past time. She enters and took a tour of the house which led her to the fireplace where she remembers the endless Christmas gatherings when life at the home was a dreamer's imagination.

"Ms Kalthrough what on earth...," the voice said and Jean turns instantly to see the face of Jeremiah standing right in front of her.

"I'm sorry I almost called you by his name," Jean said and apologizes.

"It's is no problem, Mrs Winselscott made that same mistake all the time. I even pretend to be Peter numerous times," Jeremiah said making Jean laugh. He asked her what brings her to these neck of the woods but wasn't surprise when she claim to be just passing around.

"I must be getting back as I'm expected to give care for someone in great need," she told and Jeremiah understood.

He in turn told her about his plans of selling the house but might not do so if she wants to live in it. Jean instantly decline stating it would be too much for her to make the trip to her job and back. Furthermore, it should be handed over to one of his children as they are the next in line so to speak.

"I cannot do that Ms Kalthrough as the actual owner of the house is still alive. I would have to buy it from her," Jeremiah told. He finally gave his reason as to why he has joined her and it is because he has lots of memories just like her. "I would come here just to play with Peter," he said and the two went silent for a moment or two.

The silence continued and that was because Jean couldn't help but stare at the picture left behind by Jane when she went to live with her sister. She told Jeremiah she remembered the man in the picture and remembers he looks quite dashing in his younger years. Jeremiah agrees with her adding it was the one thing he admired the gentleman for, as he too came closer then mentions he has to be heading back to the manor as he has guest who are leaving quite soon.

"Is it a lady friend," Jean asks

"No Ms Kalthrough," he said and paused for a quick second. "My guest happens to be my childhood friend George Ellsworth,"

"Sorry,"

"George Ellsworth the best friend to ex lordship Mr Charles Symmington," he replies and was instantly baffled by Jean's next move.

"I must be going," Jean said declaring it is getting rather late and she promise to be back before night fall. She didn't wait to hear what Jeremiah was going to say and heads out the door and into the taxi demanding the driver take her home with double speed.

Jeremiah could only look from the window and see the car making haste before the sun sets. He only wanted to find out if she wouldn't mind taking up residence in the house, as it is a very nice place to live, no wonder his grandfather built it on the spot it is on. He could only cast his attention towards the picture and just stare at the man inside the photo. He picks it up then quickly puts it down after realizing he too has to be getting back to meet his guest before they leave. He made one last survey and was out with the possibility that someone would find interest in the home and create memories just like the Winselscott's.

CHAPTER 35

5TH DECEMBER 1960

"I understand there are two pretend detectives lurking around these parts," Justine Meadows said to her stranger while adding the final ingredients into the well-known fruit cake. It is the one thing everyone in Cottondale looks to her for during the Christmas season, while they fall head over heels for Ms Flawington's bread and sweet treats. After she was finished to let it sit for a while she asked her visitor if he doesn't mind helping her with the tea and sandwich refreshments and heads to the living room.

"I've never before seen Jeremiah Blackworth so many times walking around here and the gentleman with him, I hardly knew him at all," she jokes and this placed a smile on her stranger's face. She finally got around to asking the name of her visitor as he looks rather handsome and quite young really.

"My name is Charles Symmington, I came here to attend the funeral of a friend of mine, former Inspector Jonathan Stonewall," he said with some sadness.

Justine could agree with him as she too claims Jonathan was more than an Inspector, he was the reason why there are police around. "It's a shame to have lost him so early, he was in the prime of his life really," she told then switch the conversation to something more lively. She is quite excited to let Charles know the sweater she is knitting is a Christmas present for her granddaughter, who will be spending Christmas with her instead of London. "Oh that's remind me,"

"Is something a matter Mrs Meadows?"

"No it's just I remembered why your name rings a bell. Am I right when I say you are the famous ex- lordship Mr Symmington?" Justine said plastering a huge smile on her face.

Charles wanted to give her the noble peace prize but instead he confesses to being the person she just identified. He even reveals smiling that one of the pretend detectives happens to be his best friend George Ellsworth seen walking around with Jeremiah Blackworth. "I was asked by Jonathan to help solve the murders Mrs Meadows, that's why I'm here," Charles said

"I'm surprise you came to me first Mr Symmington. I thought you went to the gossip sisters and got the full story," she replies making Charles love her even more.

"Busy bodies,"

"Yes Mr Symmington, those two knows what goes around Cottondale including...," she said but was cut off.

Charles finished her sentence by saying the gossip sisters knew what goes on around Cottondale including the deaths of Elizabeth Cartridge and Peter Winselscott. He even bid to differ hypothesizing that she might know something which the gossip sister doesn't have in their procession. "Now you see why I came here," he told

"I see what you mean, so I guess there is no need to keep it to myself any longer. The truth has a way of coming together Mr Symmington," Justine told then place her knitting in the chair next to her and asked Charles to join her by her kitchen window.

She drew back the curtain to display the house by the woods which to Charles was quite a beautiful house altogether. Justine gave a little history saying the house was the one thing Cedric Blackworth was quite proud of as he would visit the Winselscott's on regular bases. "I hope Mr Blackworth doesn't sell the house, as I hope to see Mrs Winselscott return," Justine said then close the curtain.

"The house looks perfect," Charles said then ask Mrs Meadows if she doesn't mind telling him what she knows.

"My story hasn't change at all Mr Symmington. Detective Browning and the inquest will see to that. Of course I was stunned to have heard of the young girl's death," she said even exaggerating a little by claiming to be horrified when the news about Peter's murder broke through. "That Sunday I was in my garden as usual attending the roses," Justine said and then move from the kitchen window to return to her baking.

Charles observed her pouring the mixture into the baking pans while listening to the interesting tale she was reciting. He was made to understand it was around the same time Conrad and his son went to the woods to do they usual peasant hunting. "Peter was a strange character indeed he was," she told and placed the cake mixture into the oven to bake, then went back to the window and told the rest of her story.

Charles did the same thing after he heard what struck out at Mrs Meadows the most form her recollection. "It was quite odd when Conrad and Peter came from the opposite direction, as their home is apparently in the woods itself. I figured they came from the home of Steven Fairbanks,"

"Why?"

"I think it had to do with the teasing Peter received from Steven. I'm not sure if Steven hated him, for all I know Steven would tease the poor lad," she told. In her own conclusion she is quite sure that Peter Winselscott might have suffered from a disease of the mind, a mental disorder so to speak. "Don't let me drift Mr Symmington; after all, you are here about Elizabeth,"

"I find whatever you say Mrs Meadows very interesting," Charles replied

"Well in that case," Justine said and went on. "Shortly after Conrad and Peter, Elizabeth walked by with a happy dazed look. Of course I asked her if she was alright and she was. I was told by her, she is off to meet a friend of hers,"

Justine took another pause to start the cleaning up of the dirty bowls with Charles lending her a helping hand. He even took the complement of being a down to earth person and how the courts of England have lost a true gem. "Why such an early retirement, you don't mind me asking Mr Symmington?"

"A personal matter Mrs Meadows," Charles replied

"Well I guess I understand but I can tell you, the only person who can sympathize with you is Elizabeth's and Peter's mothers," she said.

Charles felt left out when he learns what each mother did after their children's death. If he had done something however, it couldn't match those of Gina Cartridge who after her daughter's death made a shrine in Elizabeth's room. Jane Winselscott took to the road to deal with her grief. "I'm surprize Jeremiah Blackworth didn't do anything strange. He was quite shaken up about both murders you know,"

"I see,"

"Not only that Mr Symmington, Mr Fairbanks was acting quite strange as well. I saw him running from the woods on the same day, as if he had seen a ghost. There's one other thing I must tell you," Justine told

"What Mrs Meadows,"

"It was the time Mr Symmington; I was quite sure all of them past a little before three in the afternoon, expecting the person Elizabeth went to meet. He might have past when I went back inside," she told

If Justine knew the lights in Charles's logical mind were burning brighter than ever. She would testify to another piece to the puzzle placing it physically into his procession. All the clues began to lock themselves together, as a matter of fact Charles could reveal everything right there and then. However, you guys and gals should know Mr Symmington is much too sinister for that sort of thing. Plus, he wanted George to be the one to take all the credit.

"Is everything alright Mr Symmington?"

"Yes it is. It's just I'll have to deal with it after I assisted you of course," Charles said knowing what happen to Elizabeth and Peter.

"Thank you Mr Symmington. Now let us take a look at the cakes in the oven shall we," Mrs Meadows said.

CHAPTER 36

20th DECEMBER 1960

The tapping at the door on an early winter's morning would be the last thing Gina Cartridge would expect. She didn't mind however as it was George Ellsworth who return probably to get the rest of her story, along with an unfamiliar face with him. Immediately she invited them in but surely wanted to know what the visit was all about. "Would both of you like a cup of tea?" she asked

"No thank you Mrs Cartridge. I'm here to let you know that I'm leaving for home today,"

"And where is that Mr Ellsworth?"

"Chalfont St Peter Buckinghamshire, I'm neighbours with the gentleman with me. Let me introduce you to Mr Charles Symmington," George said

Gina became so speechless that she didn't hear her husband walk in and asked if George and Charles are relatives of hers arriving for an early Christmas visit. She ignored what he said and introduced him to both gentlemen evening confessing to meeting George a week earlier.

Reginald wasn't at all surprize, he was only interested in what the two men came to his home so early in the morning, like detectives on the hunt to solve some outstanding murder case.

"They just came to say they were leaving Reginald, no need to get all cross," Gina told

Reginald asked for forgiveness it is just he is all grumpy unless he has his early morning cuppa before breakfast. Gina told him it can wait and turns her attention back to George too ask if he had found what he was looking for during his stay.

"As a matter of fact we did Mrs Cartridge," George told

Reginald wanted in on the conversation and demanded to know what it is the men were looking for. He even compared them to the gossip sisters and made it clear the sister's will do for Cottondale's nosing around. Gina gave in and told George and Charles are investigating the murders of Cottondale and watch him heads to the window, while remembering a haunting memory which plastered itself across his forehead.

"I thought it was over when Inspector Stonewall past away,"

"Do you have anything to add," Charles asked

"No but I wish some bloody result could come out of it," Reginald snapped. He even told how his wife is reliving the horror either when another year has passed or some smart cop tries to be a hero. "We were coping very peacefully until Mr Ellsworth showed up. Now everything has return uninvited," he said

"Everyone thought Steven Fairbanks should have been hanged for her murder," Gina told,

"What about Peter Winselscott?" Charles asked

Instantly Reginald proclaim he isn't sure or doesn't care as to who killed Peter Winselscott. As far as he is concern the person did him a favour by getting rid of the unwanted thing walking around Cottondale, acting everything else except normal. "I mean he was strange and all and I guess he was just as innocent as our daughter," Reginald told

"What do you mean Mr Cartridge?" George asked then looks at Charles who nods to say it is a good question to open what the teller is trying to hold back from inside.

Reginald walks up behind the chair Gina was sitting and held her by the shoulders. She looks up and they both knew it was time to let someone know what the gossip sisters didn't know at all. "I'm surprize my wife didn't mention it to you before Mr Ellsworth,"

"I'm sorry Mr Cartridge,"

"It was something Elizabeth told me weeks before she died," he said

Again George looks at Charles hoping what Reginald might say wouldn't throw a huge twist in the case. They waited as Gina encourages her husband to say what he knows, as she watched it eat him alive for the past five years. Charles used his psychology to good use by asking Reginald to sit down so in that way he would be comfortable when he speaks about his hidden fears.

"When I found out about Elizabeth's follower, I was please to know she found someone suitable despite their age difference," Reginald told. He walks Charles and George through a day in particular when Elizabeth returned from one of her Sunday's strolls very upset. "To be honest it was shocked to be a better choice of word," he told

Charles understands it was the day Elizabeth found out the whole truth about her lover's past life and it tore her apart. "He told her about a disgrace his family carries, but he has someone who is an expert in the field to be accurate,"

"Would it be Dr Christine Meredith?" Charles said

"How did you know?"

"I had a chance to speak with her," Charles told. He further explains how he came across Dr Meredith, which led to him being a guest of hers on a few dinner invitations.

"So you know what the disgrace is Mr Symmington?" Gina asked

"The jury is still out on that one Mrs Cartridge," Charles replied keeping what he knows under lock and barrel even from George, whom is accustom to knowing way before he tells everyone. He pressed a little deeper asking Reginald the question which would surely set the truth apart from the gossip. "Who do you think killed your daughter?" asked Charles and was a bit surprized when Reginald claims to not having the answer. In fact, it was too painful to speculate any further. However, neither he nor George was prepared when Gina proclaims to have an idea as to who killed the joy in her life.

"Do you wish to tell Mrs Cartridge?" Charles asked

"That's for Mr Ellsworth to say; after all isn't he the one investigating the case?"

"Charles she claims it to by my friend Jeremiah Blackworth," George said as if releasing a dark secret, he has been keeping for so long. He also knew where Gina was heading with her claim.

"Why is that?" Charles asked

"Because Mr Symmington, on the day of our daughter's funeral, Mr Blackworth gave me this," she said and finally revealed the ace she has been holding up her sleeve for so long. Make it five years to be exact. She knew she had everyone at her mercy when she got up and went into her writing desk only to take what she knows will gave her accusation some sort of foundation. Finally, Gina showed the ring her daughter had been keeping a secret from everyone including her. She then places it into Charles's hands who then gave it to George who knew the real owner instantly. He himself finally understood what Charles has been telling him for so long, since he started looking into the case. However, it was too late now for Gina Cartridge might just have the answer everyone had been asking for the past five years.

"It was his wife's ring Mr Symmington. It should make it easier for you now, as Jeremiah Blackworth was my daughter's fiancé."

CHAPTER 37

7TH JANUARY 1961

A couple of days into the New Year but it appeared to be the same for the gossip sisters Rachel Rocksoft and Lattima Donahue. They sat in Lattima's living room and did their usual which would go down as a marked occasion to anyone who knows them well. To be truthful however everything and everyone in Cottondale had return to normal after Charles and George had returned home for the Christmas holiday. They didn't even leave a sign as to who did the awful deed of taking two lives, which by now might have been making headlines around London adding another notch under Charles's belt.

It did however leave a bitter taste in the gossip sister's mouths as they wondered why George didn't have the decency to wrap up the case in fine style. "All I can say is, we will never know the truth Lattima," Rachel said and placed the book she was reading down.

"We'll look at it this way. We can look forward to hear the thrilling conclusion in the next five years," Lattima joked making her best friend laugh heartily.

Rachel nods her head in agreement as everyone would have expected the final curtain act to have happen, leaving more questions to be answered but mostly the why. Rachel rests her tea cup down only to say what she too wanted out of the whole thing. "I thought he was the knight and shining armour who came to lift the curse from around Cottondale," she told

To Lattima, Rachel words could be taken lightly as a joke despite they were. She also felt the same way about Inspector Stonewall who was hot on the trail, and then all of a sudden everything went cold. "I think the murders are what cause him to have become quite poorly," she told but got a stunner from Rachel which hit her like a pitcher's fast curve ball.

"Forgive me Lattima, but I must tell you Inspector Stonewall past away just a few months ago,"

"Are you sure?"

"Quite really, I was there at the funeral," Rachel told also giving details as to how it went down. She first highlighted that when she went to pay her respects to the family, there was a gentleman in particular whom she had never seen before. What also made her felt floored was that the gentleman happened to be a close friend of the same very Mr George Ellsworth.

"I concluded he must have been a close friend of Inspector Stonewall as well, because when the casket was being lowered, he marches right back into the church,"

"How disrespectful," Lattima replied even stating it was utter inhumane to do such a thing. She cast it aside however when Rachel dropped a stunner when she witnessed Mrs Stonewall doing the same thing but only after the burial. "They both stayed in there for quite some time,"

"Where both of them having an affair?"

"I doubt it the man appeared to be in a different social class altogether," Rachel told

"Don't be fooled Rachel, love doesn't care who it touches," Lattima said jokily

They both laughed then went into a short pause which was the result of Lattima's pondering caused by something Rachel said. She immediately told she might have an idea as to who the mysterious man is, in the company of Mrs Stonewall. It so appears she had been reading the newspaper about a murder trial of a Mr Bentley Wright and how the man got off scot free, thanks to a well-known detective.

"Who please do tell Lattima?"

"Charles Symmington the ex-lordship," Lattima told. She describes him as being the same very man accompanying Mr Ellsworth just before they left and how they were seen entering Gina Cartridge's home on that day.

"No wonder Jeremiah Blackworth wasn't seen walking around," Rachel told and resumes her tea drinking. She lost all sense of composer when Lattima slams her tea cup and saucer against the table, then mentions there is something she just remembered.

Now the tea party was reaching the boiling point after Lattima's eureka comment. Rachel's inquisitive smile told her to spill the beans and spare none of the details. "It so happens Rachel I was in Mr Brown's store buying some produce just the other day, when Reginald

Cartridge came through," Lattima told. She found it odd as Reginald is never seen going into the store as his wife does all the shopping. Rachel was split as to why her friend found the encounter as odd, but Lattima had to bring her up to speed by claiming it has appeared Reginald has started drinking, something he has never done before.

"That's true he doesn't even want to drink the wine at the altar, but please go on Lattima,"

"Well it appears Mr Brown and Reginald had a conversation going on," Lattima said and went on. She claims to have overheard Reginald telling Mr Brown about the same Mr Ellsworth and presumably Mr Symmington who came to his home just the other night. It was like picking strawberries on a sunny, breezy day as Rachel learnt how Reginald felt like he was in an interrogation room answering questions raised by these two men.

"Oh my stars Lattima what did he say,"

"He said the man name Charles asked him if he knows who killed his daughter."

"Never,"

"Of course Rachel but that isn't the best part," Lattima said then turn up the heat on full blast, by saying the conversation went into high gear when Reginald's wife Gina came straight out with the answer.

"Are you saying Lattima the killer is still lurking around?"

"Yes and you will never believe the name she called," Lattima said and pause to give Rachel her only shot at guessing who on earth did Mrs Cartridge claims to be the killer.

Rachel nearly burst an artery not only with thinking but with suspense and gave up instantly so that Lattima could have the joy of killing her softly with her answer. You would shudder to think Rachel also had an outer body experience herself when the name was revealed to her. She couldn't bring herself to have another sip of her tea or bite of food for that matter. She just stared at her friend with wide open eyes and repeated the name to herself just to make sure she got it right.

"I don't believe it,"

"I didn't at first but from Reginald's confirmation it appears to be Jeremiah Blackworth," Lattima said

"I am just as stunned as you Lattima, and then you know what we must do. We must report this to Detective Browning. It is our duty," Rachel replies

CHAPTER 38

4TH OCTOBER 1961

Fast forward months until we once again arrive to the autumn season of the current year. It appears everything is going in favour for Steven Fairbanks, now that everyone has accepted there will be no closure for the Cottondale murders. His hard work of toiling the land is now paying off, earning him the title of Cottondale's local vegetables producer. This accomplishment has over shadowed what everyone had tagged him to be over the last six years which he is happy to forget.

He was making a usual supply stop to Mr Brown's store when Gina Cartridge walk into him, nearly making him toss the create of vegetables over. However, his quick reflexes could qualify him for England's cricket team for the next cricket world cup.

"I'm sorry Mrs Cartridge,"

"Why should you. Wasn't it me who ran into you Steven?" she said while giving assistance. After her good deed she was just about to walk away when she found the nerve to ask him a very peculiar question. "I was wondering Steven, if by chance you was paid a visit by a friend of Mr Blackworth's,"

"Paid visit, I saw him in person. Why do you ask Mrs Cartridge?"

"No reason in particular, I just wanted to know that's all," she said

Steven quickly bid to differ and asks Mrs Cartridge to come clean but gave her the benefit of the doubt, as to him she deserves to know the whole story. Gina did what Steven asks and came clean without lingering any further. She informs Steven that never once had she thought of him as having anything to do with her daughter's death. "I enforced what I've said on Mr Ellsworth right in front of Mr Blackworth," she told

Gina's statement was a bit surprizing to Steven as he always assumes she joined with the rest of Cottondale and dibbed him the Cottondale murder. He kept his guard up by not becoming flattered with her confession and continued with his delivery. He did however keep his side of the bargain by giving Mrs Cartridge what she came for. This for sure should bring some relief to her sense of mind until something new from the investigation comes along.

"I came home after meeting an old friend, only to find my mother in heavy conversation with Mr Ellsworth," he said as he continues his work

Gina felt like she was at tennis final and quickly stop Steven from going back and forth so that it would appear the two are actually having a conversation, instead of lovers having a disagreement.

"Yes I see," Gina said

"What the conversation was about I have no idea, but I figured she told him what everyone were talking about me Mrs Cartridge. I assure you of my honesty," Steven told.

"So then who did you see on that day Steven?"

"I wish I could tell you,"

"Steven please I've through enough," Gina told hoping Steven would comply. When he wouldn't budge, she decided to use the only card left in her hand, which rely heavy on sympathy. Gina reminds him of what she has been through with the only reward of endless misery. She made it clear to him how well she was coping along with her daughter's death, until the useless excuse of pretend detectives showed up at her door.

"I understand Mrs….,"

"No you don't Steven," Gina replies and continued to hammer home her pain. She hits him for six when she claims to have told Mr Ellsworth who she thinks is responsible for Elizabeth's death. "The reason why Inspector Stonewall didn't arrest you for murder is because I told him my theory," Gina said staring Steven right in the face. She also adds how her prays asked that Inspector Stonewall's soul should be never be at peace after the horror he put her family thorough. "Please Steven tell me what you know, otherwise I might have to think different of you,"

To Steven it was going way to well until Mrs Cartridge laid her cards on the table. He gave into her demand in order to avoid the threat of blackmail or it was how persistent he was with the Jeremiah that he saw also in her. "I met with Mr Blackworth on that day Mrs Cartridge," he told her

"And what did you told him?"

"I will not say Mrs Cartridge,"

Gina felt like an epiphany came over her as Steven began to let her in on the day's schedule events. As he speaks a flashback of her daughter came before her a flashback she remembers way to well, Gina came home to find her beautiful Elizabeth crying endlessly in her room after a meeting with her lover. She came out of it and cuts Steven short comparing his story to what she thought of all along.

"You know don't you Steven. You know who killed my daughter," Gina told

Steven now feeling interrogated looks to the ground as if he is about to be scold for doing something he shouldn't have. He knew he has been keeping for too long a secret, that if spoken would cast a storm over Cottondale, making it the work of the wicked witch in one of the brother's grim fairy tales. With Gina's never ending trying he gave in and told her his observation on the day her daughter died.

"I went to meet Mr Blackworth when I heard a noise. I figured it was Mr Winselscott doing his usual game hunting, but when I got there," Steven said and paused.

Gina now on the verge of finally knowing why ask Steven to carry on, even though it appears he had become lost for all words. "It was him wasn't Steven, it was Jeremiah Blackworth," Gina said

"All I will say Mrs Cartridge is that when I saw him, he had blood on his hands, then ran off when I got to close,"

Instantly Gina felt nothing at all. In fact, she is certain the ground would move from under her every time she made a step. Her mind bounces back and forth with only one question in mind. Why? Why would Jeremiah Blackworth do such a thing and to top it all off, he hid himself away behind the woods only to reappear under the protection of George Ellsworth.

"I'm going to the police,"

"No Mrs Cartridge,"

"It has been too long Steven. I entirely blame this on Inspector Jonathan Stonewall for allowing this to have happen," she said. She thanks Steven then turns and began making her way home only to stop as the knife ripping thoughts began tearing at her stomach. Through the mix of it all Gina felt that some relief has been reach through her encounter with Steven. She also wishes she could crumble like a cookie but couldn't as having justice for her daughter had become her ideal focus. "It is time this matter is settled once and for all. The truth must be spoken," Gina said out loud and continue making her way home.

CHAPTER 39

25TH OCTOBER 1961

It was just short of eleven o'clock when Charles and George found themselves walking down the popular street of Seville Row. Charles was on an errand to his tailor and had asked George to tag along while he has final alterations done on his custom made tailored suit. "I've been invited as an honoured guest of Lord Eustace Kingston's fifty third birthday party,"

"You must be looking forward to it Charles,"

"Quite right you are George, we were once Harrow boarding school prefects, before I met you," Charles replies and point with his cane to Augustus Cashton's tailored store.

Once entered Charles was immediately ushered by Mr Cashton and his assistant into the dressing room to change, then place right in front the mirror. George laughs at how Charles was treated like a mannequin with his extremities being toss in all directions. While Cashton and his assistant waste no time in making final alterations to Charles's suit, he took the chance to asks George if he had taken the time to go through all the evidence he gathered while in Cottondale.

"I glad you've have asked that Charles. I actually did some thinking and might have a plausible theory," he replied

"Well let's hear it," Charles answered then nods his head to Augustus to say he is satisfied with the adjustments made to his suit. He was very impress with George who told a very solid theory but somehow felt that things aren't as clear as they should be. Charles found himself on the same page as George who also mentions there are a few questions which are left outstanding.

"What puzzles me the most Charles is everyone has their own story but isn't clear as to who murdered those two persons,"

"How do I look George," Charles said then turns and faces George hoping to get the ultimate comment out of him.

"Where you listening Charles,"

"Of course George I heard everything you said perfectly, but what I can tell you, there is more than one lead character in this play," Charles said then gave the okay again to Mr Cashton.

George was a bit stunned by Charles's early conclusion. He knew he followed Charles's methods by the book but yet came up short by a mile. He was then told to switch places with Charles so that Mr Cashton and his assistant can also make final adjustments to his suit as well.

"I don't understand Charles how come I'm going. I thought you were taking Dr Meredith with you,"

"I am taking her, but I somehow manage to persuade Lord Kingston to allow me to bring an extra guest," Charles said. He did however spill the truth and told George, how scared he was of taking another chance at love.

"Of what Charles,"

"At finding love again George, I'm a forty-nine-year-old man and Christine is quite young really,"

"So what"

"Call me paranoid but I am worried what people might say George,"

"You have never been secure before Charles,"

"Explain," Charles replies and sat to listen to his friend gave a lecture on love and its rewards.

Don't be fooled by Mr Symmington. It is true he has never felt insecure as it was him who chased Martha down until she agreed to marry him. It was the perfect distraction for him to do some deep thinking about what George said earlier about the case and would use it to build a more logical theory around the unanswered questions. The first was just as George claim, as none of the stories told pointed to a solid motive. This is why on his many tips to Inspector Stonewall's bed side cozied with his men having difficulties about arresting Steven Fairbanks on the suspicion of murder.

"The case has a twist that I can't see Charles," he remembered and that is what was needed to bring Inspector Stonewall's theory closer together.

Charles on the other hand had enough clues which point the whodunit clearly but he is beside himself of actually telling George the truth. His reason why he is holding back is because he knows who the killer is and quite agree with Inspector Stonewall when he visited his bed side for the last time. Lastly it is important to George that he speaks with his childhood friend Jeremiah, if he is to see the truth and the direction the case is pointing.

"George a lot of speculation has been cast from the beginning," He told George

"Why could you say that Charles, when the one sure thing was Steven Fairbanks being seen before and after Elizabeth's murder,"

"True, but didn't you find it peculiar that Steven Fairbanks only went to the woods, whenever Elizabeth went there," Charles replied

"What are you getting at Charles?"

"I figure Steven Fairbanks might know who Elizabeth's killer is and is holding it to ransom," Charles told. He went a bit further by informing George that Cottondale might hold the final piece of evidence he is looking for.

George gives the okay to Mr Cashton then turns his attention again towards Charles. He clearly told Charles he is putting him into an awkward position. Charles admits to it by insisting that George truly speaks with Jeremiah Blackworth as he fears there is something Jeremiah isn't telling him.

"George I always wondered why Jeremiah took you to see Mrs Tallbottom. There is something interesting I fear,"

"Charles, Jeremiah wouldn't lie to me. He already told me everything he knows and I for one believe him," George made it clear

"No George," Charles said then asked George to concentrate deeply on all that he knows and he would find none of them seems to be adding up. "What I'm saying George is that the stories you've heard are in fact the story," Charles told then he made his biggest slam dunk since he took up the case. "Trust me George when I say the biggest clue was given when everyone including ourselves wasn't paying attention," Charles said.

To George, Charles has done the unthinkable right under his nose. He was stunned to find out that the blood hound is close to solving the six-year-old mystery. One thing for sure he isn't going to let Charles have his way with Jeremiah Blackworth as he still believes his friend has nothing to hide. Call it naïve but it is the simple case of support for anyone you made history with. He looks at Charles and knew for a fact that certain things still don't add up.

"Charles what are you saying,"

"Yes George. The answer I am looking for is what has been left behind. I must return to Cottondale alone,"

"I see Charles,"

"However I will leave you to go over your theory in great detail," Charles said then gave Mr Cashton the amount to cover the delivery of the suits. He then turns to George and confess straight out that he would never try to come between him and Jeremiah Blackworth. However, he fears that if George doesn't speak with his friend a greater mishap lies in store for them both.

"George I beg of you, please to please confront your friend Jeremiah. Otherwise what I might say will be the end of our friendship," Charles said and left George alone with his thoughts.

CHAPTER 40

27TH OCTOBER 1961

Dorothy came down the stairs in a hurry and that was due to her awaking rather late. She heads directly for the dining room and was greeted by Christine who was already having breakfast with her brother Donovan. She apologizes for her tardiness but Christine writes it off, claiming she can't remember the last time she did anything as a family with Donovan. She looks at him with a smile on her face, and then told Dorothy she wouldn't be teaching her class today, as she is taking the day off.

"I don't understand,"

"No need to, let's just say you will have the day to yourself, but I would need you to look after my brother this evening," Christine said. She became very excited to tell Dorothy why and waited for her to have a seat. Immediately Christine showed a letter she receives from her parents and another person with some very good news.

Dorothy too became quite excited and thought the idea of eating breakfast while listening to good news is quite a thrilling idea. She was glad to hear Christine's parents had written to her but was more interested in the person who is responsible for Christine's morning glow. "Would I be right if I guess the person as Mr Symmington?"

"Right you are Ms Twinkleton he invited me to be his guest to one of his friend's fifty third birthday party."

"Who,"

"Lord Eustace Kingston,"

"I'm happy for you," Dorothy said then begins eating quietly which appeared to be a bit odd to Christine. She was then asked if something is wrong and wouldn't mind saying why. Dorothy place her fork down then wipes her lips with the napkin and gave her answer hoping it wouldn't offend Christine in any way. "It is just Dr Meredith I gets rather unsettled whenever Mr Symmington's name is called. Don't get me wrong, I want you to find love but….,"

"But what Ms Twinkleton, I can assure you Mr Symmington is not interested in what you have to hide," Christine replies in a rather upset tone. She even confessed to Dorothy to have told Mr Symmington what she knows including the story surrounding her friend Jane Winselscott. Realizing how she had lost her cool with Dorothy, Christine became sympathetic and made amends by ensuring there will be justice for her friend Jane Winselscott and the horror that came to her son. "Stop your worries Dorothy e….," Christine tries to finish, but the maid interrupted her to say there is an urgent telephone call that awaits her in the hallway.

With haste Christine rush through the hallway with countless uncertainties dancing through her mind. At first she thought something dreadful had occurred in South Africa and the authorities were calling to notify her. Her nerves might reach for the ceiling if it turns out that Mr Symmington was calling to say he wouldn't be able to take her to Lord Kingston's birthday party. She answers the phone with high expectations only to find out that none of the above isn't compatible with what she is about to know.

"No it can't be," she said to the person over the line. Nothing could have prepared her for this. It was as if giant boulders were rolling over her at top speed which made it the more horrifying. "Have you contacted your solicitor?" she asks.

"No," she heard.

"Then I shall notify him at once and will meet both of you there," Christine said and drops the phone in order to save herself from falling over by leaning against the wall.

The sudden outburst made Dorothy rush into the hallway to ask what the urgent matter was. She understands from the look on Dr Meredith's face, some major crisis had just occurred that no one was prepared for. Again she asks Dr Meredith what the matter is and was about to get the details full blast when Christine turns away from her to look at the root of it all.

"I'm sorry Dorothy,"

"Dr Meredith please tells me what happen," Dorothy said with just as much panic as a herd of zebras running away from a pride of lions. She couldn't believe what her ears had just heard and she too turns for support by sitting in a chair close by.

"The call was from Jeremiah Blackworth. He has just been arrested on the suspicion of murder," Christine said and watched the tears began to flow from Dorothy. She tries to comfort Dorothy who now feels more helpless than ever before.

"Everything is going to be fine,"

"No it isn't Dr Meredith; the fear has come to past, and I'm afraid for my friend Jane more than ever,"

CHAPTER 41

27TH OCTOBER 1961

It seems like ages since Jeremiah Blackworth has been sitting waiting in a prison cell. How he got into this mess can only be explain thoroughly by the arch angel Gabriel. His frustration made him rattle the bars hoping to break free but it was no use as he wasn't a descendant of Hercules. The noise somehow attracted detective Browning who came in like the king pin of the playground.

"Ah Mr Blackworth we were just about to come to you,"

"There's no need to, I don't belong here,"

"Well justice thinks otherwise," Detective Tommy Browning said then turns to constable Thorne Tripe to guard the door while he has a talk with his suspect. Constable Tripe did what was asked of him and once he left Detective Browning waste no time in reading Jeremiah his rights and what he might soon be charge with if Jeremiah co- operates nicely. He got straight to the matter at hand by stating a mysterious visitor came to the station with some very interesting information about the deaths of Elizabeth Cartridge and Peter Winselscott murders. "They claim to have been living with the knowledge the whole time,"

"That's hogwash Detective Browning and you know it," Jeremiah said trying to keep his cool.

"That's not relevant Mr Blackworth, I considered it as a breakthrough in my murder investigation, and don't you agree," Detective Browning told

Jeremiah got up and pace the floor while thinking how did it all came about. He broke his silence by asking Detective Browning who on God's green earth would put him up to such nonsense. Detective Browning turn the table around by encouraging Jeremiah to give a complete statement, then hire the most expensive solicitor to defend his innocence.

"I have nothing to defend. I already claim to have not done those hideous crimes," Jeremiah replies

It was Detective Browning's turn to go silent; he did so as a way to calm himself from pulling Jeremiah Blackworth through the bars by his neck. What made him angrier was the selfish constant denial Jeremiah kept claiming, when he could just come out with it and save himself from the long drawn out murder trail which might take years to prepare. Detective Browning decided to play good cop by asking Jeremiah if he doesn't want to see Gina Cartridge have the peace of mind she deserves. She might even go as far as to forgive him for making such a mistake but will have the strength to carry on, since she has been portraying excellent coping skills for over six years.

"Please Mr Blackworth just tell us why you did it and prepare yourself to ask Mrs Cartridge for mercy,"

"I swear…,"

"No, no, and no that wouldn't do. You know why?" Detective Browning said then dove right into his reason. He rekindles Jeremiah's memory by asking him if he remembers the late Inspector Jonathan Stonewall. When no response came he went on with his history lesson by forcing down Jeremiah' throat how he watches the late Inspector Stonewall worked day and night trying to solve the case. "As I said he worked day and night, I tell you, until his illness came of course," he spoke in a much softer tone.

What he wanted to see more than anything was to see some remorse comes from Jeremiah face, so that he could take the long journey up to Inspector Stonewall's grave and tell him how the case was solved. To him Inspector Stonewall would finally have that long vacation but up where angels fly until the break of day. While Detective Browning speaks Jeremiah Blackworth did some thinking of his own. He went through everything that had occurred over the last six years. Worse of all he is afraid of what his only friend George Ellsworth might soon find out and crush him into a million pieces. Right there and then Jeremiah knew there is only one solution to it all. It would save everyone from the torture while he reaps the rewards of not having to face them to give an explanation including Elizabeth if she was there.

"Alright I give in," Jeremiah said and saw the smile on Detective Browning's face which he believes it was the story which did the trick.

"Good the courts should me merciful on you,"

"I can't run form it now," Jeremiah told

"Run form what?" Albert Tesslington said cutting off any celebration Detective Browning might have after Jeremiah's written statement. Albert a man around the same age as Jeremiah but a bit shorter walks up to Detective Browning and hands him his card. He told the detective he is Mr Blackworth's solicitor then gave a scolding to the detective saying he should know better than to drag a confession from any potential suspect without a decent solicitor present. He then introduces Dr Meredith who just walks past everyone and heads directly for the cage which holds Jeremiah captive.

While Detective Browning and Albert Tesslington argue over the rights of the suspect, Christine and Jeremiah use the time to come up with a logical reason as to why they are here. She learnt from the start that Jeremiah is ready to confess and there is nothing no one can do about it. Christine asked him if he is going directly out of his mind, or has being behind bars did the trick to send him into insanity. Jeremiah walk away from her but Christine demanded that he stays put so that they could work themselves through this mountain pile of a mess.

"I can't take it anymore Christine," Jeremiah told

"How could you, everything is at stake can't you see that Jeremiah?" she replies. She felt applaud when Jeremiah states the charade has gone way out of hand but she reminds him that Dorothy's friend Jane Winselscott is going to face a horrible time if he decides to confess. "You didn't think this thing through Jeremiah, and you didn't kill those people,"

"I know that Christine but the prison is making it hard to believe," he replies

"You need to keep your promise Jeremiah; you owe it to Jane,"

"I believe you are out of bounds Dr Meredith," Detective Browning said

"Am I right when I say he is entitled to at least one visitor," Christine snaps but was stop by Albert when he asked her to let him handle the detective. She complied and step away from Jeremiah hoping he would understand the look in her eyes and keep his promise.

Detective Browning asked Albert what kind of stunt he is trying to pull but Albert backlash when mentioning that he could have influence his client in making a confession without proper protocol. He even smiles when he says it would be a slam dunk for him when he tells the presiding judge what occurred and have the case thrown out even before prosecutor Briggs could start.

"Enough all of you," Jeremiah told making everything come to a screeching halt. "That wouldn't be necessary Mr Tesslington, I've made a decision," he said and read how stump they all were which gave him the upper hand he needed to get what he wants.

"I don't understand Jeremiah," Christine said

"Neither do I Mr Blackworth," Albert said looking at Christine with a blank stare.

"I will confess but only in the presence of Mr George Ellsworth. It is him or nothing at all," Jeremiah said then sat on his prison bed without a care as to who accepts his negotiation deal.

To Detective Browning it was the most bazar thing he has ever heard in his line of work. However, it might give him the information he needs to finally get the case solve. He looks at Albert who just shrug as to what to say next, then to Christine who just walks away after feeling betrayed by the party. He then recalls constable Tripe into the room and consulted with him and when finish he returns his attention back to Jeremiah. "It has never happened before, but I am willing to go against my principles and allow this met to happen, but I want everything," he said in frustration.

"Very well Detective Browning. I will confess to the murders," Jeremiah told then looks at his solicitor knowing very well he has nothing to lose.

CHAPTER 42

28th OCTOBER 1961

With the morning newspapers claiming readers by the miles, there was no doubt as to what the cover story is all about. It surrounds the capture of the Cottondale's killer which would be the perfect article to read while having breakfast on a chilly autumn morning. Mr Brown paused right on the doorsteps of his shop just as he was about to open for business. He looks around to see if anyone else is just as stunned as himself, but it appears it was no apparent surprize as villagers assumed it all along. A regular visitor to the shop stops by to purchase a paper on his way to work at the factory and instantly sense something is wrong.

"What's a matter Mr Brown?"

"Jeremiah Blackworth has been arrested,"

"On what grounds,"

"Murder," Mr Brown told but managed to see one other person was just as surprize as he was. The visitor name Clyde Talltree made one suggestion which would haunt Mr Brown for quite some time, or at least until the murder trial is over.

"Well at least Gina Cartridge got her wish. She has been saying so all along,"

"Why is that?"

"She always hated him and only she knows why," Clyde said and was on his way

"I see what you mean Clyde," Mr Brown said to himself and watch Clyde continues on his way without any concern.

"Oh my," were the words of Mrs Meadows who sat at her dining room table unable to take another sip of her tea. She rushed her mind back to the visitor she had late last year and the discussion they had. "I hope," she said wondering deeply if her visitor was the one responsible, as she read the part where the police claim that someone had information concerning the death of the two murdered victims.

Justine placed her hand to her mouth absorbing how the police also claim to be baffled when the murders first took place but thanks to new information the case is well on its way to be solved. She had to pause for a moment after her mind derailed from the thought of the killer acting out a fantasy and worse they might have idolized one of England's most notorious killers Jack the ripper. Mrs Meadows became instantly floored when she saw the picture of who the killer is, and hopes the paper wouldn't be faced with a lawsuit for making such a disaster of a mistake.

"Why I never, how could it be," she said and was lost for all words. She quickly began rethinking her story with her visitor as she always assumed Jeremiah Blackworth was always a good boy at heart. Never once would she imagine Jeremiah to have such intensions and what caused it should be something of interest should psychologist investigate.

"I'm adamant of the person I saw running away from the woods. It was Steven Fairbanks," she said to herself until something which had skipped her mind before forced its way back into her thoughts. "He showed no interest the second time otherwise I would have seen him," she said and knew the whole thing doesn't add up. Mrs Meadows got up and again heads to the kitchen where she looks at the Winselscott's home, then the field before the woods and it was there it all came back to her.

Of all of the surprize readers of the morning you would be surprize to know Rachel Rocksoft and Lattima Donahue tops the list. In fact, they found the story more thrilling than a late night movie on a Saturday night. Rachel came over just as soon as she caught eye of the story which would be the bases for a good gossip discussion with her partner in crime. "Jeremiah Blackworth is the Cottondale killer. How?" she asks.

"Serves him right I had a hunch it was him. He was acting rather peculiar on the day that man Mr Ellsworth had tea with us," Lattima replies

Rachel quickly defends Jeremiah by saying it is much to puzzling to her to think Jeremiah could do anything like that. She argued he never showed any signs of inappropriate behaviour and would allow anyone to enter the woods unlike his grandfather. She was then challenge by Lattima who asks why she would say such and gave her reason as to why.

"Lattima the Winselscott's moved in shortly after Cedric Blackworth made his intentions clear, but yet they were free to enter," she said where Lattima had no other choice but to accept Rachel's statement as reasonable doubt.

They cast it aside until Lattima again slam her tea cup and saucer against the table and shouted out a name as another possible reason. "Gina Cartridge,"

"I'm sorry," Rachel told

"Gina Cartridge remember she had sheer hatred for Mr Blackworth. I think it was her who went to the police," Lattima told

"Not Mrs Cartridge, Lattima,"

"The devil and sin are best friends Rachel. Jeremiah just happens to be a cousin of theirs and Mrs Cartridge found it out," Lattima said jokily. She quickly wipes it away after Rachel asks the question which everybody around Cottondale should be asking themselves, which was if Mr George Ellsworth had already read such words about his friend.

"Let's wait and see Rachel. Mr Ellsworth might just come to his rescue; after all he never gave us his theory on the matter. So now might be his chance" Lattima said and of course Rachel agrees with her.

Gina sat on her shrine Elizabeth's bed just staring at nothing despite the curtains serenade her like a song thanks to the wind that blew through them. She was taken off her wondering from Reginald who walks in and rests his hand upon her shoulders and felt the warmness of her skin. He asks her if she had by chance read the morning paper and was a little surprize when Gina said she did.

"I'm glad the police have him, that's why I came up here," she told.

"I'm glad it's over. At least it wasn't by those two men who prove to be worthless idols," Reginald replied. He also said that if it wasn't for that mysterious character Jeremiah Blackworth would be walking around laughing heartily.

"He could have left her and found someone his age," Gina said then faced her husband "It was me Reginald, I'm the one responsible for his capture,"

"Why Gina,"

"Because he deserves it that's why and I have no remorse," she replies then began crying.

Reginald presses her against his chest only to hear the bottle up of emotion of six years. He miscounted the ways in which his wife declares her hatred for Mr Blackworth and it was the sweetest sound he had ever heard. "It's alright my darling you don't have to be afraid anymore," he told her while looking to the ceiling and thanking Elizabeth for pointing to the truth, something her parents had been looking forward to for some time.

Wanda quickly calls to Jane and asks her to come down stairs and joins her in the kitchen. Once Jane appears she wastes no time in telling her what she read in the morning paper and what they have as their headline. It was surprizing to Jane as she took the paper and read it for herself then looks at her sister with worried eyes.

"I never expected anything like this," Wanda told

"Don't be because it's all a mistake, I assure you," Jane replied

"I believe you," Wanda said. She listens as Jane insists it was Steven Fairbanks who did such a horrible thing and not Jeremiah who couldn't harm anything which breathes. Wanda came to her senses and agrees even more with her sister and looks at her sister who just stared blankly across the room. She calls to her twice until Jane returns to her senses and apologize for her absent mind ness.

"I'm sorry sister dear I just remembered something,"

"Jane aren't you a bit worried, I sure am. If Jeremiah confesses to the murders then they will come looking for you,"

"I'm not worried Wanda and please let them. A person like me isn't afraid after what I have lost. Chances are I might have something which they might want to hear," Jane said then got up and heads back upstairs to her room. She lies upon her bed and just stares at the ceiling.

Wanda follows her and stands in the door way and looks at her. She found herself wondering what it is her sister is thinking about. Her biggest fear would be to come to her sister's room and witnessed her own sister had taken her own life. She walks a little bit closer but was stop by Jane who told her to stay where she is put and come no further. "I'm worried Jane about everything,"

"Then there is only one person to blame is there, now leave me alone," Jane replies then close her eyes and drifts off hoping it will all go away once she awakens from the nightmare she is having.

CHAPTER 43

1st NOVEMBER 1961

THE NIGHT OF THE PARTY

Everyone would testify that the presents of Charles Symmington was the ultimate birthday present for Lord Eustace Kingston. He was the toast of the crowd when he spoke about the mischief he and Charles got into while being school prefects at Harrow's boarding school for boys. "Charles do you remember the time when I place a frog into the desk draws of Mr Campsnapple our history teacher," he said and laughs the hardest.

"Yes I do, you were given lines immediately and had to give up cricket for a week," Charles replies and raise the level of laughter to a whole new level. He looks at Christine who laughs along with everyone else but became infatuated with his sense of humour. He quickly glances over in George's direction who wasn't at all interested in anything and he knew why. It was just as the gossip sisters had feared George had read the newspaper about the arrest of his friend Jeremiah Blackworth. This was a major concern for Charles as he has never seen George in this type of situation before. He was distracted for a brief moment when another joke by Lord Kingston was made and he of course had to take part.

Eventually he excused himself from the clutches of merriment and heads in the direction of George, leaving Christine to continue to embark in the celebration. "George you must pull yourself away from this,"

"Don't try to lecture me Charles, you know I cannot do such," George replied. He confessed to Charles about being right all along and now he is burden with the thought of not speaking with Jeremiah when Charles told him to do so. "Charles I assure you Jeremiah is not a murder," George said then adds his own story to the case. He told Charles about Jeremiah's rough upbringing during childhood which is responsible for him being so reserve but he was the only member of the Blackworth's that was well respected.

"Charles I know this may sound strange but I need your expertise to help solve this matter. Everything I have learnt and feel has clouded my emotions,"

"I agree with you George that's why I have decided to return to Cottondale alone," Charles told. If he has never saw what love for a friend before in someone's eyes then he was Happy to have seen it in George, making him feel the same way about their friendship. He now understands why George wanted to solve this case as he wanted more than anything which was to prove himself right about standing by Jeremiah. He also knew that everyone sooner or later would point the finger at Jeremiah and cast him to the hangman to be slaughtered without ever once giving him the benefit of the doubt. "I now see how important this case is to you George," he said then told George to be prepared because of what he found out at Summerset House. He then insisted George remain at home until he has it all figured out, where he will then reveal it for all to hear.

"George give me at least two days that's all I ask,"

"No Charles I prefer you to tell me right here, right now. Is Jeremiah Blackworth the Cottondale killer?"

"I cannot reveal that now George I….," Charles said before he was cut off and interrupted by a team of five headed by a person well known to Christine.

Lord Eustace Kingston became instantly outrage and asks the leader of the group on what grounds does he have on his premises, as his party was by invitation only. "I won't apologize for doing the crowns work Lord Kingston. I only came here to speak to a Mr George Ellsworth,"

Did everyone felt taken back? No everyone was thrilled to see the blood hound and his sidekick were about to make history on some overdue murder case. Lord Kingston began to smile and turns to ask Charles if a game of whodunit was his birthday present to him. "I hope it is me and I'm prepared to let you use me as your guinea pig," he said and everyone laughed.

"I assure you it's nothing of the sort," Charles replied

The leader of the five who now had enough of the charade identifies himself as Inspector James Whitehall and his invited guest is Detective Tommy Browning from the Cottondale's police station. He explains they are here on an urgent request to speak with Mr George Ellsworth on an important matter.

Lord Kingston finally understood what the matter was all about and points to the gentleman standing next to Charles.

"Thank you," Inspector Whitehall said and heads over to the two gentlemen where Charles introduce himself then steps aside to allow the Inspector to carry out his duty.

For a brief moment Inspector Whitehall was excited to be in the presents of the two most highly respected men in England, but had to control his excitement by remembering what he came there to do. He quickly calls Detective Browning who came forward and waste no time in informing George as to why he is summoned.

"Do you know a Mr Jeremiah Blackworth, Mr Ellsworth?"

"Yes I do,"

"Well then I'm here to inform you that Mr Blackworth has been arrested and charge for the murders of two people and is ready to confess,"

"I know I read the papers,"

Again everyone was super and highly thrilled except for Christine who already knows the story. She became secretly embarrass by the way at how her friend Jeremiah is being dragged across England like the biggest spectacle since the queen's coronation. She looks at Charles and knew she can't stay and be torn apart any more, and then quickly made her exit by slipping through the crowd hoping not to be seen by either of the Detectives.

Charles now understands how George feels stood helpless as he too is now torn apart with the summoning of his friend and the chance of obtaining love for the second time. If that wasn't bad enough he also fears he might lose them both with the knowledge he has on the two murders. He cast his own feelings aside to continue to listen to Detective Browning telling George that Mr Blackworth is ready to give his confession but will only do so if he is present. He walks passed Lord Kingston who finally gets the message that the matter is more complicated then he imagined and heads outside where he sees Christine standing at the bottom of the steps trying desperately to wipe away the tears from her eyes.

"Christine,"

"Don't come near me Charles," she said but it was no use as he came and stood right in front of her.

Charles wanted to hear from Christine why she ran out in such haste, which would give the impression that she is guilty of something. He assures her he is on her side but Christine stops him dead in his tracks while staring into his innocent eyes.

"No Charles it is just as Dorothy said. It's time for the truth," she said

CHAPTER 44

Christine took the handkerchief Charles gave her and dried her eyes. She turns away from him to allow herself to gather some confidence then told there is something she wanted to add to what was said on the evening she invited him to dinner. Charles allows himself to become empty of all his thinking and allows Christine to have her way.

"I'm glad you allow me this chance Charles, as I have made the decision not to see you again," she told.

At first Charles thought the hands of fate is being unfair but truthfully it is. How could it allow love to waltz back into his life then was ready to take the first train out even before he had a chance at tasting its sweet nectar from the flower it blossoms. "Are you listening Charles,"

"Yes I am,"

"Well you would remember the day of Bentley Wright murder trial, when I became cross with you after Lordship Fairmount passed his sentence,"

"Go on Christine,"

"Please Dr Meredith, anyway," she said and started her story. She reveals she was in the continuation of looking for answers concerning her brother's medical condition when she first met him at the library. "It wasn't all Mr Symmington I was also there to finalize my conclusion on another patient of mine," she told

Charles couldn't believe what he knew all along as Dr Meredith confessed to knowing who the patient was all along. He found out the patient had similar findings to that of her brother which was why she attended the trail just to get a better understanding at how the behaviour works. Her confession not only stunned Charles but also cause him to feel the brunt of a break up when in love. He continues to listen as Christine filled in the blanks of the curse of her family and how it affects at least one of them in every generation.

"When my grandfather found out it instantly broke his heart which lead to his death. It came from his side of the family as his eldest brother named William was the first to have signs,"

Charles wanted more than anything was to grab Christine and pulls her to him and be her knight and shining armour. It faded just like a dream when Inspector Whitehall burst through the doors of Lord Kingston's manor followed by his group of men and George in the mix of them. He knew time was running out and asks Christine to finish what she started but Christine ran away from him and stops Detective Browning and begins another conversation. He felt a deal was made when she gotten into the same car as George and Detective Browning and drove off without one ounce of goodbye to him. He was then joined by Lord Kingston who immediately asks him if he isn't going along with his guest, but could clearly see Charles wasn't invited.

"Why Charles aren't you going to follow them?"

"Not at all Eustace; I was hoping it would have happened this way," Charles said with a smile on his face trying to hide what he is feeling on the inside. He told Eustace he must excuse himself from the party and promise to make it up to him over a game of cricket. He quickly went to his car and drove off after the valet brought it around and drove off heading in the direction of the place where the final pieces are hidden, and will show everyone how good they were at being wrong.

CHAPTER 45

29ᵀᴴ OCTOBER 1961

Velda Sweetroum opens her door only to realize it was a surprize visit from Jean Kalthrough and stops her afternoon activities instantly. She could think of endless reasons as to why Jean made the unexpected visit but toss it all through the window just to find out what's new with her best friend.

"I would have called but I figured the news have to tell should be told in person," Jean said and was led into the sitting room.

"Is it about the murders? And would you like some tea," Velda asks

"It won't be necessary as I am not staying long," Jean replies.

Velda jumps at the chance and got the conversation going saying how shock she was to found out it was the most prominent man in Cottondale. She even quires if anyone in the village ever saw him acting in peculiar fashions and was stunned to find out no one even took notice.

"I assure Velda Mr Blackworth isn't that sort of man," Jean told

Velda took Jean's answer as the final word and tries to change the subject to something most interesting but couldn't. She asks Jean if she remembers the last conversation they had with Mrs Tallbottom. "Of course I remember,"

"Well you have heard when she says the killer had to be someone in disguise,"

"I don't remember her saying that,"

"Oh I'm sorry weren't you there?" Velda said and somehow had second thoughts as she is quite sure Jean was present when Mrs Tallbottom mentions the words.

Jean felt like a child at story time as Velda went on about what she and Mrs Tallbottom spoke about when she wasn't there. It was quite entertaining as she learns Mrs Tallbottom and Velda were playing the game of detective. "I remember her saying she wouldn't be surprizing if the killer was someone close to the girl she said," Velda told and giggle. She also mentions how surprize she was to have found out it was the person who cared for the girl the most after reading yesterday's paper.

"And he is ready to confess the nerve of him,"

"That's enough Velda," Jean snapped. She couldn't stand anymore of Velda's and Mrs Tallbottom's wild imagination and then states what her main reason for coming over too her house. "I only came here to tell you that I have accepted another position and wouldn't be able to see you any longer,"

Velda was stunned plus shocked and floored all at the same time. She asks Jean why and was even more taken back when Jean just say she is ready to move on and there is nothing anyone can say to change her mind. "My position is in America Velda. A place I always wanted to go, a good place to forget about Jane," she said.

Velda was certain that for once in her life the cat surly had her tongue. She just sat there and stares at Jean as if looking at her deceased grandmother that came back to life for just about a minute. "I don't know what to say Jean,"

"Say that you are happy for me," Jean told.

Before Velda could say anything she quickly notice the watch on Jean hand that she was reward at Mrs Tallbottom's will but cast it off to wish Jean good luck. "Will it be long?"

"Yes. I plan on taking up residence there it should be my new start on life,"

"Then this is goodbye then,"

"No. It is just the hands of time has a way of changing someone's fate I gather," Jean told in a sadden tone then got up and makes her way to the door. As she makes her way down the steps she didn't look back and that was because she didn't want Velda to see the sadness in her eyes. She would however take along all the memories she gathered while visiting but for now she is happy to take the opportunity to move on.

Velda stood at the door and watch her friend of only four years makes her way down the driveway of her home. She felt a bitter sweet emotion came over her as she knows it is the last time she will see or hear from Jean Kalthrough again and that was heart breaking for her. She did wonder for a brief moment as to why Jean didn't look back at her, but figured it would be best, as looking back might make her stay into a life she doesn't mind leaving behind.

CHAPTER 46

2ND NOVEMBER 1961

With the mid-morning being in favour for a cosy snuggle under the covers, it would be the last thing on Mr Symmington's mind as he races against time, now that a threat of a confession is due at any moment. He arrives in Cottondale unannounced and immediately heads to Mrs Meadows who was more than thrilled to see him. She felt less worried after finding out it was him who went to the police and again took him to see the home of the Winselscott's from her kitchen window.

"I'm glad you came again Mr Symmington and I hope you find favour in what I'm about to tell you,"

"It would be my pleasure," he replies and listens to Mrs Meadows before heading on his way.

As he walks the small distance Charles began to reflect on every clue he received since he took up the case. The most recent was the clue given to him by Dr Henry Whistlelite another friend of his and who is an expert in human behaviour at Oxford University. He learnt that a person with such behaviour would be scene as unbalanced because they wouldn't be able to separate reality from friction during an episode. It all made sense to him when he took what he researched and the conclusion from Dr Meredith and joins them together to actually see the back stage view from the medical perspective.

Next he took all the findings from George and Inspector Stonewall and was able to place together what would be the final nail in this overdue case coffin. He couldn't forget the shock he encountered while paying a visit and this was the reason why he kept his suspicions under locking key. All of the above couldn't compare to what Charles found most valuable while asking a favour at Summerset House.

He saw the house as he came up the walkway where a gentleman stood waiting like hours for him to arrive. He stops mid-way to look at the house in more detail and had to admit it was a cut above the rest in the village. It would be a dream paradise to anyone who has their sights on owing their own home, complete with a lovely garden in the front and a view which stretch across as least five acres. At the end of the view stood Jeremiah' manor castle, but what took Charles by surprise was the woods which stood to the right of the Winselscott's home, which he doesn't mind visiting.

"Are you the gentleman who is interested in buying this house?" the man's voice shouted from the porch.

"Yes I am," Charles shouted back.

"Well come along then," the man's voice return and watches Charles made his way up the steps, with a little knee trouble.

The man introduced himself to Charles as Mr Albert Tesslington and is also the solicitor for Jeremiah Blackworth. He explains how

Jeremiah became the owner of the house after the previous owner's widow, took up residence with her sister in Cheshire.

"Please to meet you Mr Tesslington,"

"I must inform you that I am in rather of a hurry as I have an important matter to attend,"

"Well let's get along with it, shall we," Charles joke and follows Albert into the house.

Once inside the house Charles look around and became very impressed with its décor. He cast away the apology from Albert about Mr Blackworth not been able to make repairs which is due to a pressing matter.

"No need to worry my wife and our staff will see to its tidiness,"

"Where is your wife Mr...,"

"Mr Cage but Mrs Cage had an urgent matter to attend as well, don't worry Mr Tesslington i have brought homes before," Charles said while exploring the home from room to room.

It didn't appear odd to Mr Tesslington about the through search of his potential buyer was making. He observes how Charles searched behind every wardrobe and cupboard draws as if looking for something in particular. "Is everything to your specification Mr Cage?"

"Of course my good man I just wanted to make sure they took everything," Charles said jokily. He even took it further by saying he doesn't want anyone banging down his front door, while he is entertaining himself with his sympathy music playing on Sundays.

"And what about your wife, sir,"

"She will be in the kitchen doing the one thing she loves more than me. Baking," Charles told again and begun laughing so too did Mr Tesslington. He then asks to see the rest of the home where Albert was happy to comply.

After the inspection of the kitchen which was to Charles satisfaction Albert finally took Charles into the living room to have a look around and hope he would make an offer before the sun disappears. "Are the phones working Mr Tesslington?" Charles ask

"Why yes they are Mr Cage, the bill notes are paid through the estate of Mr Blackworth. Oh that remind me I must make a call to say I will be rather late," Albert said and left Charles to continue his inspection alone.

Like a lion on the verge of a successful hunt Charles began looking around. He took a look through the window which showed the rest of Cottondale that appeared to be miles away. He admitted to himself that the house does carry a very nice view all round including the view of the woods from the kitchen window. He was interrupted by Albert who states he just return to see if an agreement could be reach but was a dunce when he stood right in front of the answer Charles was looking for all along. He was asking by Charles to give him a few more minutes to think things through and complied even though it appeared odd too him.

Charles trod carefully over to the fireplace and stared at the priceless clue like he was in a trance. He took it up as if it was the world's most valuable piece of art and instantly all the puzzle pieces began locking into place. This was what was needed to help Inspector Stonewall but he never saw it standing right in front of him. Charles knew and could explain the one thing which was nagging away at Peterson Castries's mind and the final clue Jonathan left for him at his funeral. He also thought he receive an additional bonus when he looks from his prize and stared at the picture that was probably left behind.

"It all makes sense now," Charles told himself as he configured the final chapter to this story which he truly dubbed "The hands of time."

"Again I must apologize Mr Cage I didn't know they left it behind. I will contact them immediately,"

"It won't be necessary Mr Tesslington. It will come in handy," Charles replied. He then asks Mr Tesslington if he will be representing Jeremiah Blackworth while he gives his confession.

"Why yes I am. Why do you ask?"

"I wouldn't disclose my querying. However, I want you to do me a favour,"

"Very well Mr Cage but what is it you ask,"

"I want you to delay the proceedings of the confession,"

"Mr Cage,"

"It is important that you do," Charles stern words hit Albert with a much unexpected blow to the ribs.

If Albert didn't know better, he would swear the man looking at him is a prominent lordship of some sort. He didn't understand why this figure would ask such a thing when all he was interested in was to make an offer on the house despite an announcement hadn't been place in the newspapers.

"Please Mr Cage I might lose my license,"

"If you want your client not to hang for murder, then you must stop Jeremiah Blackworth form giving the confession," Charles said then gave instructions as to go about it to Albert, while he sets another master plan of his into action.

"You say the phone line is still in operation?"

"Yes sir,"

"Good now go and do what you are told. Delay the confession," Charles said and watch Albert sped off as if he had just seen the ghost of the headless horseman. He quickly went into the hallway, picks up the phone and dials the operator. She answered and Charles requested her to patch him through to line 6372 and waited with impatience. Once the butler answered the line he immediately asked to speak to Lord Kingston.

"Lord Kingston speaking,"

"Eustace this is Charles, I need an urgent favour of you,"

"Please go on Charles,"

Write down these instructions," Charles told and begun laying out the plan that will shed the light on the most cleverly planned case he had ever come across.

"Charles I will see to it right away," he heard and hangs up the phone as he awaits the work of Albert in order for his plan to pull through.

CHAPTER 47

4th NOVEMBER 1961

The day of reckoning had finally arrived, the moment of truth so speaks. With all that he had learnt plus the strong friendship with Charles on the line, George was ready more than ever for the truth. He sat next to Detective Browning but couldn't tell anything about him as his eyes locked dead and center with the biggest mystery he is about to know, the mystery of Jeremiah Blackworth.

He wanted to say something but couldn't as it might jeopardize his chances at being able to put his theory together. This was something George wasn't going to allow too past through his fingers. A quick glance around and George saw the face of the lady Charles has been speaking about and figured she was there just like him to get the whole story. He had to admit she is one attractive lady and he doesn't see why Charles would want to miss out on his luck. He also concluded that Christine is there just like him to give her friend some support and even might find interest after this storm blows over.

He listens as Detective Browning addressed everyone present by saying they are only there to listen to a confession that will bring an end to the Cottondale murders.

"Are you ready to begin Mr Blackworth," Detective Browning ask

"Yes I am," Jeremiah replies then looks at both Christine and George and physic himself up to reveal what everyone has been dying to hear. He took another look at Christine and read instantly what she was trying to tell him, while a storm of uncertainty causes him to look away from George.

"I'm ready," he told but that would be all he was going to say.

No one was prepared for what was said next that even had Jeremiah stunned to the core. What is this? He questions, after all he didn't want George to come all the way over here to be insulted. He wanted to win back his friend George and at any cost to himself for that matter. Jeremiah looks at his solicitor who figured he had just been bestowed with the power of boldness and wanted to know if he was willing to share what inspired him to do so.

"I cannot allow this confession to take place," Albert said and begun packing his briefcase.

"Is there a reason Mr Tesslington," Christine asks but was relieved to know that Jeremiah would be stopped from making a fool of himself.

"Yes there is a reason which I will not disclose with you at this moment," Albert replies then took out what appeared to be invitations after packing his briefcase. He gave each of them their own including Jeremiah before giving instructions that he must heads straight home and speaks to no one until the date written on the invitation. "You are free to go Mr Blackworth bail has been made," he said the stops to give them a little teaser as to why he did what he did.

"As I was heading to my car to make my way over here, I was approached by a man who just gave me these," he said and asked everyone to take a look at their invitation.

"It says we are invited to a house warming dinner on the 5th which is this Friday," Detective Browning said even disclose the charade as rubbish. He did however tell Mr Tesslington that since his client had gone back on his word he is more than happy to see to it that Mr Blackworth spends the happiest days of his life behind prison bars. "By the way when I find out who is responsible I will see to it that the culprit gets what he deserves. Twenty years for interfering with police protocol,"

"I assure you the person responsible has claim on the truth not your eye witness," Albert said

"My eye witness will testify against Mr Blackworth where all will be told,"

"Your so call eye witness is none other than Gina Cartridge,"

"How did you know that?"

"Attend the dinner party Detective Browning and furthermore I want to hear what this person has to say. Until then I forbid my client from making a confession," Albert said then signal to the guard to take Jeremiah straight home as he is under his supervision as of now. He then walks out of the room without having one ounce of pity toward George whose main interest was to see Jeremiah clears his consensus and faced whatever fate come his way with his support of course.

"I'll guess I will see you both at dinner," Christine said and follows Albert who felt a new phase of existence had invaded his body.

George knew way too well who is responsible for such an act and took another look at his invitation. He instantly realized his invitation wasn't an invitation at all, instead all that was written on it was a world which read "Friendship" and he knew that Charles Symmington is ready to reveal what he knows.

"I'm sorry Mr Ellsworth," he heard Detective Browning said and left and knew first hand that if new evidence comes up the police must first check it out to see if it is of value.

"I wondered who knew it was Gina Cartridge," Detective Browning said as he left the room which was about to help him crack the biggest case in Cottondale and his career history.

George quickly placed the invitation into the envelope and left the police station to go to the only place where he knows the truth will be serve by the master chef himself Mr Charles Symmington.

CHAPTER 48

4ᵀᴴ NOVEMBER 1961

Lord Kingston felt like a teenager again as he speeds down the road heading towards Cottondale. He had just completed what was asked of him and was even more thrilled at the part he played in his friend's master plan. His topless ford sport car came to a stop where he met Charles at the foot of the steps of the home he supposedly brought.

"You should have been there Charles," he told in a very hyper mood as he got out of the car and joined Charles to see how well his house servants where getting on with the decorations.

As they entered both were impressed with the décor of the rooms and the transformation effect it will have on the guest tomorrow night. They examined every room but came to a standstill once their entered the living room where the story of all stories will be told.

"I see everything went according to plan," Charles said

"Of course Charles everything went like clockwork," Eustace replied and began to give a through description of how it all unfolded.

His tale begins with his arrival to the solicitor of Jeremiah Blackworth and how he almost went paler when Eustace gave him the invitation and instructions and laughs very hard. "You should have seen his face when I told him I am working for a private detective," Eustace told with more merriment than the fans of Liverpool after winning a major football league championship.

Charles on the other hand wasn't at all interested in any merriment. He just wanted to show there was more to what the gossip sisters knew, that would be responsible for the breakup of a friendship between Jeremiah and George. He bounced back and listens to Eustace who overly enjoy the fun he was having when he visited the homes of Wanda Chestnut, Velda Sweetroum and Dr Christine Meredith, whose live in lady look more panic when she accepted her invitation.

"I see tell me more,"

"Of course Charles," Eustace said becoming a little bit more serious when he mentions he will never forget the look on the lady's face as she too became pale when one of the invitations had her name written on it. "Somehow Charles I felt for her,"

"Quite," Charles replies and taste a slice of the pound cake to be serve as desert after the main course.

"Make sure you have the best bottles of wine ready Rupert," Eustace told his butler and continued. "All the other invitations were delivered on my way back here Charles," he told

"Of course and thank you," Charles said and watches Eustace heads to the kitchen to take a well deserve lunch for a job that was well executed. "Excuse me sir where do you want this?" he heard and turns only to see Rupert holding a small grandfather's clock in his hand. "I will take that," he said and took the clock and heads directly to the fireplace.

After placing the clock next to the picture which was left behind on the mantelpiece, Charles took a step back and saw how well the three bland together. The clock against the picture that stood underneath the major clue should do the trick to explain what happen in Cottondale all these years ago. Despite he has it all put together there is one person whom Charles would have love to be present Inspector Jonathan Stonewall. He was the main contributor to solving this mystery as Charles remembers the last clue Jonathan left behind and knew it was what was needed to make his theory picture perfect.

"Charles we must get some rest before tomorrow night," Eustace said and observe for a brief moment the soft side of the blood hound.

"Of course we should. Truth waits for its grand entrance," Charles said as he looks at the completed story of Elizabeth Cartridge and Peter Winselscott.

CHAPTER 49

5TH NOVEMBER 1961

Just as you read from the beginning of this story the guests accepted the invitations without any second thoughts. They gave the host their highest approval on a job well done and embanked themselves on topics of their leisure before joining their host in the living room for a story telling like none other. Mr Symmington took his place by the fireplace and looks at the clock, then to the picture before turning to face his guest.

"I not only invited you all here for a house warming dinner but to bring an end to what happen in Cottondale six years ago," he started and locked eyes with all that were present.

"So you are the one who is responsible for the odd occurrence yesterday at the police station," Detective Browning told.

"It's Mr Symmington, ex lordship Charles Symmington to you Detective Browning," Charles told in a stern voice and began his introduction. He told everyone he is quite sure that only a few of them might know who he is in detail except for George who sat next to Gina

Cartridge and her husband Reginald. He complemented everyone for looking so dashing looking at Jeremiah who looks way better in his own attire than the clothes the prison offers. He got right to it and also mentions that the gathering is one person short, the only person to have known the truth but fate has its own agenda.

"You mean my husband the late Inspector Jonathan Stonewall,"

"Right you are Dorielle," he said and went on. He reveals to them it was the late Inspector who first introduced him to the details surrounding the murders of Elizabeth Cartridge and Peter Winselscott who died two weeks later.

"Haven't we got the killer? I'm quite sure the police have the right person," Gina said looking with every hatred expression found in the book at Jeremiah.

"Quite right; we were about to get the confession before all of this happen," Detective Browning states then told his constables that they are going to leave, as they were only invited to a dinner not a stage performance.

Charles would now show who is holding all the cards when he throws the first nail into coffin by enlighten that the confession Jeremiah Blackworth was about to give was going to be a lie. He looks at George who just had blankness written all over his face but Charles knew it is the only way the truth of the matter must come to light.

"A lie Charles, are you sure?"

"Indeed George the confession which Jeremiah was willing to reveal, was to protect a secret at all cost," he said knowing his statement would cast a new complexion on the mystery. In fact, Charles had dropped a bomb shell to be more precise.

Everyone felt as though they were thrown off the band wagon but Lattima makes the first try to get back on by asking Charles what it is he is talking about as there is no secrets kept in Cottondale.

"Is it true Jeremiah?" George asks before looking into his friend's eyes who sat on the opposite side to him. He knew at this point Charles couldn't be lying as it appears he has all the aces in his hand and no one can escape from the theory which is about to come.

"Don't say anything Jeremiah," Christine intervenes and she looks at Charles as if he had just torn her heart out of her chest.

"I'm sorry George the confession was to stop you from knowing the truth," Jeremiah said and looks to the ground. While there he had another moment to think about it all. It was like a pain that wasn't going away and now that someone is ready to relieve him from his torture he is more than ready to face the music. He raises his head then looks to the one person who also would want the truth be told, from the only person that saw through the cloud the murders have gathered over the years.

"Please Mr Symmington I will not stop you now," he said and allow Charles to do what he does best.

Charles walks up to the fireplace and takes up the picture then walks back and hands it to George who looks at it then again looks at Jeremiah who is now ready more than ever.

"The gentleman you see in the picture is that of our grandfather Cedric Blackworth," he said

"Grandfather,"

"Yes, Jeremiah and I are both cousins along with," Christine said and stops as it wasn't her story to tell well at least not yet.

"Along with who Christine," Gina Cartridge said after realizing that what she knew was completely opposite to what is being said now.

"Along with Peter Winselscott," Charles told and absorbs the stunned faces before him. He looks first at Rachel and Lattima who went into numbness and wouldn't feel anything if pricked with the world's sharpest sword. He then cast his vision to Steven Fairbanks and his mother who just remind speechless just like when they arrive. The most fatal of all was George who felt as though he was being beaten with whips every time something interesting is said.

"Why you never told me this Jeremiah?"

"Because Peter was born around the same time as Gina's Elizabeth," Dorothy spoke for the first time about her friend's past.

Now that Charles has everyone by the hook he would now clear up an old wife's tale that Rachel and Lattima has encouraged from the beginning. He asks George if he remembers the story the gossip sisters told him during his investigation on the case. Immediately George corresponds with Charles but became lost for words when Charles told the gossip sisters forgot to mention one minor detail.

"We never forgot anything, I was a close friend of the Blackworth's," Rachel told

"Then you would have known their entire history," Charles said as if scolding her for something she should have kept plastered at the back of her mind. "I made the visit to Summerset House to ask a friend a favour during my investigation. It was there I discovered the valued piece you forgot," he said to Rachel and went on. "It is true that Cedric

Blackworth was married before his second marriage to a lady by the name of Jacqueline Winselscott. When he divorced her for his second wife Jacqueline took with her their only child a boy by the name of…,"

"Conrad Winselscott was the uncle to both Jeremiah and Christine. Yes, Conrad was the first born of Cedric Blackworth, my friend Jane told me all about it," Dorothy told cutting off Charles which he didn't mind because he is getting quite close to the person whom he wants to help him complete the final chapter.

"When Jacqueline returned to her place of birth she wanted to erase all history of her son's rightful inheritance," Dorothy told then hands it over back to Charles.

"Right you are Dorothy, Jacqueline ask her friend to change the last name on a new birth certificate for her son, changing his name back into a Winselscott. However, she kept both birth certificates where she would use to her advantage at least for one last time,"

"When Conrad became of age his mother wrote to his father telling him about Conrad's marriage to my friend. It was there Cedric Blackworth built this house next to the woods, as my friend Jane his wife was already pregnant with his son," Dorothy told taking in the smile of the blood hound himself.

To everyone it appears Dorothy and Charles was doing the dance of the flamingo. They couldn't believe that Dorothy knew everything about the Winselscott's and the Blackworth's putting to shame the gossip sisters who should have aced this part of the story from the beginning. Dorothy continues and recited everything she knows even when her friend told her about the strange happens of her son Peter, which she was afraid to tell not even Cedric Blackworth.

"He was such a good boy," she said

"How do you know all of this Ms Twinkleton?" Eleanor asked her then turning in time to see Charles facing the fireplace once more.

"When Inspector Stonewall became ill he did one other thing that surprized me," Charles told and went on giving the details on how his friend continued to work on the case, while battling his illness. Detective Browning who now started to see the light of day confirms the blood hound's claim by stating he met with the late Inspector on numerous occasions.

"Which brings me to my biggest clue yet," Charles said. He told everyone that on visits to the Inspector's home, Jonathan reveal certain clues including the one on his death bed. He hits home stating it was at Jonathan's funeral that his wife Mrs Stonewall came with a message that cast everything into the light.

"He said to ask her," Dorielle told

"That's right Mrs Stonewall; your husband finally knew who the Cottondale killer was,"

"Are you saying the killer is a woman Mr Symmington?" Detective Browning ask

"No Detective Browning. Inspector Stonewall was telling me to ask the one person who knew it all," Charles said and pause and looks at the person he had his eyes set on from the moment they arrived. "He was asking me not to ask Dorothy Twinkleton or Jean Kalthrough. He wanted to ask you, Jane Winselscott," Charles said with a checkmate smile.

CHAPTER 50

Silence was like a warm blanket on a cold autumn's night as everyone looks at Jane Winselscott for the first time in six years. However, Charles wasn't finish he was just warming up. He asks the butler to send forth another guest of his whom he had asked to come hours before the dinner then asked that they stayed upstairs until he was ready for her. When the person walks in they were stunned to find out the truth as they were listening from behind the door.

"You are not Jean Kalthrough," Velda Sweetroum said and looks at Charles absolutely stunned to the core then was ask to take a sit as there is the rest of the story she wouldn't mind hearing. After Velda took her seat Charles turns his attention to the mental history of a patient of Dr Meredith by the name of Pauline Wright.

"She was a patient of mine that's why I made sure I was present at the trail," Christine said

"What does that have to do with anything," Detective Browning asked impatiently.

"Do you mind Detective," Lattima said then insulted him when she mentions it appears he haven't learnt anything so far and also becoming more intrigue with the blood hound.

"The illness of Mrs Wright was that of the same of Peter Winselscott," Charles said and moved up hill from there. Everyone came to understand that when Cedric Blackworth's older brother acted with the same behaviour as Peter, it was what was responsible for Peter's death. "The seeing of illusions, having constant medical attention and the uses of water and impaired speech were all too familiar to you right Dr Meredith."

"Yes Mr Symmington my uncle, brother, Peter and Mrs Wright were all victims of the mind disease schizophrenia,"

"True but Peter was the worst of them all,"

"Yes Mr Symmington my family begs you," Christine said as she begins to cry. It was more than she could stand, where she got up to leave but was stop by Jane who found the courage to say the words Charles wanted to hear from the beginning.

"It was my husband," Jane said and pause then looks at Charles, then to Gina and finally Jeremiah the one person she turns to after what happen but kept him blinded over the past five years. The one person she hurt most of all. "Conrad Winselscott is responsible for taking the lives of both Elizabeth Cartridge and our son Peter. I am dreadfully sorry," Jane said unable to say her son's name. She drops into the chair and was assisted by Christine and the others who ran to her side.

Gina on the other hand wasn't too happy and instantly told there has to be a mistake as Conrad Winselscott is now dead. She continues to say it is Jeremiah Blackworth and got the backing from Steven Fairbanks who finally let everyone knows he saw the whole thing unfolded. Little did he know Charles was waiting for his chance and told him that what he witnessed was the after effect of the incident that took place.

"I swear I saw Mr Blackworth running from the woods with blood on his hands,"

"But you also forgot that Conrad Winselscott also made the trip to the woods. You used what you saw to wrongfully blackmail Mr Blackworth," Charles said leaving Steven in a humiliated moment.

"Why Mr Symmington, Elizabeth cared for Peter," Gina said softly

"There wasn't any reason Mrs Cartridge because the death of Pauline Wright and your daughter is jointed together by the motive some solicitors use to cast reasonable doubt,"

"Are you saying Charles that Elizabeth was killed by accident,"

"That's right George it was an accident," Charles said then knew it was time to write the final chapter now that all the loose ends were tied up. He turns to Jeremiah and returns the favour by asking him to tell the story of his beloved tragic end.

Jeremiah accepted then turns to Gina first and swore he would have never hurt her Elizabeth as he truly loved her. He could only hope she would accept his peace offering then turns to George hoping that a friendship such as theirs is worth telling the truth for.

"This is my true confession George, this is what I should have said to you from the beginning," he said then stops and got the all clear from George who looks at Charles who nods his head then back to Jeremiah.

"On that fatal day, Elizabeth and I were planning to meet at our favourite place in the woods. A place I still visit today. We agree to meet earlier that day and not at our usual time,"

"Elizabeth left around 2:30 that afternoon. She was so happy that she forgot the ring you gave her on her night stand," Gina told as she is finally coming to grips with the truth.

"Yes that's right I saw when she passed. It was shortly after Conrad and his son went into the woods after coming from the opposite direction," Mrs Meadows said and knew she done well when Charles smile at her. Steven Fairbanks then told Conrad came to his house and accused him of teasing his son because of his condition.

Jeremiah continued with his confession when he told George he had asked Elizabeth to marry him the day before. He even chuckled to pondering at how he was going to ask George to be his best man. Finally, everyone saw the tears for Elizabeth began to flow. Tears that Jeremiah wanted to shed for so long but couldn't as he found it hard to let her go. He also told how Steven Fairbanks knew about the two of them and just like what Mr Symmington said he used it to blackmail him.

"However Steven forgot that Conrad my uncle and his son also came to the woods and it was there that Peter had one of his episodes. He mistaken her as an illusion and when Conrad was about to shot a peasant, Peter swung him around and he shot her dead instantly. I race to her side but I was too late she was gone. I ran away after Steven saw me and believe I killed her. The next day Conrad and I met where he confessed to me. I'm sorry George," Jeremiah told after his moment of grief had past.

The next thing he felt was the hands of Gina and Reginald Cartridge who again finally understood their daughter was in love with the man of her dreams. Reginald did something that not even Charles saw coming. He walks over and takes Jane by the hand making her stand to face him. She felt he was going to do something drastic as everyone was prepared in case of such an event. However, he didn't do anything drastic instead he took the clue from Inspector Stonewall and use it to his own advantage.

"I now know what happened to my daughter Mrs Winselscott. Now I am asking you to finish the story by telling us what happen to your son Peter Winselscott,"

CHAPTER 51

To Charles it was the defying moment of his case as he watched Jane Winselscott walks up to the gun that completed the puzzle pieces to help solve the mystery. She touches it and instantly the hatred memory returned to her but at least she is ready to face the hurdle in her life, she was ready to let go of her Peter.

"After what Peter did, Conrad wouldn't be able to stand what might happen should the truth be found. Every day he became paranoid that he would leave our home with the gun to go to the woods to kill himself and if anyone asked why he did it. I was to say he couldn't live with himself for killing the young Elizabeth,"

"Would I be right when I say it was you who told him what to do," Charles said knowing that the only way Jane can have the closure she wants; she would have to confess to the part she played.

"Yes Mr Symmington," she replied then turns to face him. "I told him there is only one option left that he must,"

"That he must take a life for a life," Charles said and from there he finished the story by asking Jane to carry on by looking at him and pretending that he was Peter. Jane did just that and invasions Charles as her son.

"Two weeks after the death of Elizabeth Cartridge, I made Peter his favourite meal stuff peasants wrapped in bacons and cream potatoes. When he was finished, I got him dress and watch as he and Conrad walk through the door and into the woods, knowing that only one would return to me. Conrad told me he took him to the same spot then told him to look at a dear that was passing. He took a few steps back aimed and fired just as Peter was about to turn t him to say the dear wasn't there," Jane said and truly started to grieve. She found comfort in Charles's arms as they all heard her say "I've killed Peter; I've killed my baby,"

Charles looks at George then to Detective Browning and nods his head to say it is all over and close the book that took everything including the lives of everyone it engulfed. He hands her over to Velda who despite felt betrayed couldn't turn her back on a friend whose only guilt was to run away from a horror of a nightmare.

CHAPTER 52

7ᵀᴴ NOVEMBER 1961

Two days after the storm of the case had past Charles realize there was something else left to be done. He found himself standing over the graveside of the late Inspector Jonathan Stonewall and thought of the moment when he would finally be able to truly tell Jonathan what he wanted to know for so long. He wouldn't have it any other than to be alone with Jonathan, as George is spending a few more days as Jeremiah's guest and is a frequent visitor to Ms Flawington for her breads and sweet treats, which he had the pleasure of enjoying.

He starts off by telling Jonathan how he was left with a complete knowledge of the case and will now polish off the rough edges of the story. He told the complete version of the story with the confessions of Jeremiah Blackworth and Jane Winselscott. Anyone that was there walking along the cemetery would be convince by the way Charles went into detail about how he solved the case.

He first enlightens the grave by saying how it was the case of Bentley Wright that got the whole mess going. He told how Pauline stepped from behind the door and unto one of Bentley's tools, where she unbalanced and fell to her death. He couldn't wait to tell Jonathan the plan Jeremiah and Christine cooked up by first finding some elderly person such as Mrs Tallbottom who needs looking after, where Jane under an assume name such as Jean Kalthrough would take care of her and when she died Christine would take her on as Donavan's house sitter.

He gave more details how they switch Jane's name to Jean then using the last name of Jeremiah's mother's maiden name to create a new name so that Jane wouldn't be mistaken if she sees someone she knows. They did however switch the name to Dorothy Twinkleton and got Jane's sister Wanda to go along with the idea when she visits her in Cheshire, where they would only know the true identity of Jane Winselscott.

"I knew it was her when Wanda made the mistake and called her Jane and when I saw her at the dinner party of Dr Meredith's," he said

Charles saved the best part for the last when he told the grave how he believes that after Conrad confessed to Jane about the murders before he died. He then told how Jane then confided in Jeremiah about what his uncle did, who then confided in Dr Christine Meredith. He also did give the downside of the case and told the grave how Christine had kept her word of not wanting to see him anymore. She had decided of taking up a teaching post in America and will be taking her brother Donovan and the same Jane Winselscott with her to start a new life. However, Jane would make calls to her new best friend Velda but the grave would be happy to know she would be using her real name.

"In all I'm glad you asked me to help you on this case. I never thought it was so rewarding to be back after I lost Martha and now you. I hope both of you are looking down at me smiling," Charles said giving one last joke about the gossip sisters. He told the sisters are a lot quieter and everyone seems to joins them for tea including Reginald and Gina Cartridge who uses the friendly gossip to past the time.

"Thank you Jonathan as I have a cricket score to settle with Lord Eustace Kingston." Charles said then places a flower on the grave and made his way out of the cemetery.

THE END

MR SYMMINGTON IN: HANDS OF TIME

WRITTEN BY: COREY HOWARD

DATE: 12TH FEBUARY 2017

REEDITED 30TH APRIL 2017